Thom Braun w
Hackney and W
to St John's College, completing a PhD on Benjamin Disraeli at University College London, he worked at Birkbeck College, London University, and at the National Enterprise Board before joining Unilever in 1982 as International Affairs Manager. In his nine years with Unilever, he was also Lever Brothers' first European Brand Manager, and then a General Marketing Manager and Business Group Chairman at Birds Eye Wall's. Since 1990 he has worked as a marketing consultant – a job he combines with his writing and his role as an ordained Church of England priest. He lives in Surbiton, Surrey, with his wife, Jill, and their two sons.

Also available by the same author

Holy Orders

Free Spirits

THOM BRAUN

Marshall Pickering
An Imprint of HarperCollinsPublishers

Marshall Pickering is an Imprint of
HarperCollins*Religious*
Part of HarperCollins*Publishers*
77–85 Fulham Palace Road, London W6 8JB

First published in Great Britain
in 1996 by Marshall Pickering

1   3   5   7   9   10   8   6   4   2

Copyright © 1996 Thom Braun

Thom Braun asserts the moral right to be
identified as the author of this work

A catalogue record for this book is
available from the British Library

ISBN 0 551 02973 0

Typeset by Harper Phototypesetters Limited
Northampton, England
Printed and bound in Great Britain by
Caledonian International Book Manufacturing Ltd, Glasgow, G64

For Alec and Edward

Contents

No Escape

You hem me in, behind and before, and lay
your hand upon me. Psalm 139

'ARE you sure you know where you're going?'

By way of reply I gave Cheryl one of my more withering looks, and swung the car round a long left-hand bend.

'This road looks familiar,' I said, slowing to about ten miles an hour.

'That's because we drove along here two minutes ago,' said Cheryl tartly. After eight years of marriage, only two things could be relied upon to start a row. One was trying to hang wallpaper together. The other one was the general topic of navigation on those occasions when we were travelling in the car. So long as we were not in the car *together*, then Cheryl's navigational skills and my driving complemented each other perfectly. I remembered the occasion six months before when Cheryl had saved me on the day of my ordination at Southwark Cathedral. Finding myself lost and without a road map, I had called Cheryl on the car phone, and from home she had been able to relay directions to where I was marooned in the middle of a south London industrial estate.

I was about to remind my wife of this, but she was already ahead of me.

'What's her phone number?' said Cheryl, wrenching the car phone from its mooring. 'Mrs Whatsername?

What's her number? I'll give her a ring and find out where she lives.'

'Her name's Mrs Clubb. She's only been coming to St Mary's for a couple of months. I met her for the first time at the newcomers' party, and I don't know her phone number. But I drove her home once after an evening service in Lent so I know where she lives,' I said patiently. 'That is, I'll know it when we get there.'

'When you get there?' Cheryl said. 'I think I'd know the pyramid of Cheops if you stuck me in front of it – but that doesn't mean to say that I'd know how to drive there!'

I tried to ignore the note of sarcasm. Cheryl's next interjection, however, startled me.

'There!' she almost screamed at me, pointing to a man who was crossing the street.

'It's all right,' I said placidly. 'Calm down, darling. I missed him by a mile.'

'No, you clot. I was pointing out who it was,' she sighed. 'It was Frank.'

'Frank?'

'Frank Foster. Don't tell me you've forgotten who your churchwarden is. It was Frank. He must have been going into Mrs Whatsername's.'

'Clubb,' I said.

'Clubb, Chubb, whatever her name is,' said Cheryl. 'Turn round and go back.'

'I can't turn back or stop here. It's a narrow road. I'll have to go round again.'

Cheryl sank down in the passenger seat next to me and looked up imploringly at the roof of the car.

'Great religious leaders of our times,' she said. 'Number forty-eight, the Reverend Michael Dunn – non-stipendiary clergyman and advertising agency account director – whose famous quotation summed up the spiritual plight of the church: "I'll have to go round again". Round and round. Round and round. In ever-decreasing circles.'

There was no point in being cross for long with Cheryl. I glanced across at her and allowed myself to smile as she warmed to her theme.

'I can just imagine you,' she continued, 'changing the course of religious history with your sense of direction. Standing next to Moses in front of a huge unscalable rock face saying, "I can see it's a mountain *now*, but on *my* map it says 'the Red Sea'."'

'OK, OK,' I said, giving in to the inevitable. Cheryl, however, had not finished.

'I can imagine St Paul embarking on his journey to Rome with *you* steering the boat. Three months later he fetches up in Arbroath, and generations of Christians find themselves studying his Epistle to the Caledonians.'

'Enough!' I cried as I reversed into a space outside Mrs Clubb's house. While I was climbing out of the car, however, an incident from my day at work came back into my mind.

'Talking of Scots,' I said, looking at Cheryl across the top of the car, 'what would be your reaction if one of your students gave you three bottles of Scotch?'

'Some chance!' Cheryl replied. 'Why do you ask?'

I was about to explain, but I could see Mrs Clubb advancing down the garden path towards us, a large and threatening smile spread across her face. There was clearly no escape.

'I'll tell you later,' I said under my breath, shepherding Cheryl towards Mrs Clubb and our evening with the Jubilee Circle.

The Jubilee Circle was a group of people who met on a regular basis to discuss topics of one kind or another, to hear visiting speakers, or to visit local places of interest. The members of the Circle were drawn mainly from the congregations of the two churches in the parish, St Mary's and St John's, and meetings were usually held in people's homes. The Jubilee Circle had been formed in 1977, and had taken its name from Queen Elizabeth's Jubilee. At its founding the group had included parishioners of all ages, but as the years passed the membership had grown steadily older so that, by the time Cheryl and I were invited to talk to the Circle, we were by far the youngest people there.

It was a Thursday evening in late April, barely six months after my ordination as a deacon in the Church of England, and it appeared that some of the people of the parish were intrigued by the thought of having an advertising man as their part-time curate. So it was that we arrived at the house of Mrs Belinda Clubb to speak to the group on the subject of 'The life of a new clergy family'.

As we sat down on two ornate pink chairs either side of a grand fireplace, I looked at the faces that were turned in our direction. Several of them I knew very well. Colin Grey, the verger of St Mary's and a veritable thin stick of a man, especially without his cassock. Doreen Butcher, looking her usual pugnacious and floral self. The two Marys, Mary Brown, glamorous as always and appearing to wink at me injudiciously, and Mary West, in her redoubtable brown everything. Frank Foster, the churchwarden of St Mary's, and Joy Bartholomew. Then there were John and Rose Burgess, whom Stephen Pickle (the priest-in-charge at St John's) and I commonly referred to in private as 'the Prophets'. In addition to these worthies, there were three faces which were familiar from church, one person I hadn't seen before, and, of course, Mrs Clubb herself.

Mary Brown, Honorary Secretary of the Circle, opened the proceedings.

'Friends and neighbours, members, fellow circlers,' she began. Frank coughed and turned the colour of beetroot.

'We are honoured this evening,' continued Mary Brown determinedly through the coughing, 'to have with us the Reverend and Mrs Dunn – Michael and Cheryl – to speak to us on the subject of "Redemption – is there hope for mankind?"'

'Not redemption, Mary,' said Frank gruffly, having recovered something resembling his usual colour.

John Burgess chimed in at this point in his usual prophetic way.

'No redemption! Oh woe!'

'No, he means it's not Redemption *tonight*,' said Doreen with a deadly serious air. 'You remember, Mary, we said we would hold over Redemption until another time, so that we could fit in Michael and Cheryl.'

Mary's cheeks turned a subtle shade of pink and she fluttered her eyelashes menacingly at the assembled company before fixing her green contact lenses directly on me.

'Oh, Michael,' she crooned. 'I *do* apologize. I was reading from the *old* programme. Redemption indeed! I'm sorry, everyone. What I *meant* to say was that Michael and Cheryl have come here this evening to talk about, to talk about . . .'

'The life of a new clergy family,' prompted her companion-in-arms, Mary West, looking up from her notebook with her familiar dour expression.

'That's right,' agreed Mary Brown, her face a picture of rapturous vacancy. 'So. Over to you. Michael and Cheryl!'

Cheryl glanced sidelong at me with an 'Oh, dear!' look in her eye.

'OK,' I said. 'Can I begin by saying how pleased both Cheryl and I are to be here.'

'You *can*,' said Rose Burgess loudly, catching me rather off guard.

'Right,' I said, realizing that this was not going to be as straightforward as I might have imagined. 'Thank you, Rose. Well, you're probably wondering how an advertising agency account director came to be a clergyman in the first place.'

I peered around the room at the semicircle of faces, none of which betrayed any particular confirmation of my opening comment. Suddenly a voice said, 'Mr Cousins who used to live just off St Mary's Road was the director of something in social services.'

There was a tantalizing silence, before I said, 'Yes, thank you, Joy. Anyway, as I was saying . . .'

Oh yes. It was going to be a long evening.

* * *

Ten minutes later I had finished outlining my thoughts on 'The life of a new clergy family' and was about to hand over to Cheryl, when Mary Brown waggled her head coquettishly at me and intimated that she wanted to say something.

'Yes, Mary?' I said, reacting to the waggling.

'I just wanted to say, Michael, how much we all think about you.'

She looked around for some general support but her gaze was met mainly by looks of gentle incomprehension.

'That is,' she corrected herself, once more turning a subtle shade of pink, 'that is, how much *I* think of you.'

At a stroke she had claimed the rapt attention of the

whole group. Doreen even leaned forward in her chair.

'No,' squeaked Mary, turning a rather darker shade of pink this time. 'I don't mean I think of you in *that* way. That is. What I meant to say was . . .'

Her words tailed off into a somewhat incoherent gurgle.

'I think what Mary's trying to say,' added Mary West, looking up from her pad, 'is that she *prays* for you.'

'Yes, yes, yes,' shrieked Mary Brown, feeling that the cavalry had arrived. 'I pray for you. I pray for you. I don't *think* about you. I *pray* for you. That is, I pray for *both* of you. Yes, both of you.'

'Well, that's very kind of you,' said Cheryl, managing to look serious and concerned.

'Indeed,' I added. 'And, of course, we pray for you as well, Mary.'

Whilst this seemed, at that precise moment, to be a good thing to say, it had the effect of plunging the meeting into a morass of mutters and counter-mutters as everyone turned to his or her neighbours to assure them that they were being prayed for.

At the end of this rather desperate exchange of well-intentioned simpering, everyone seemed exhausted by the effort and the group fell into a short silence, at the end of which John Burgess intoned deeply, 'But who will pray for the rainforests?'

I looked around warily only to catch the eye of Doreen Butcher who said robustly, 'Carry on, Michael.'

'Righto,' I said chirpily.

'Can I ask a question?' came a soft voice from the back. It was a distinguished-looking older woman whom I had seen before on only a couple of occasions.

'Of course,' I said.

'Izzy Hutchings.'

'Is he what?'

'Izzy Hutchings,' said the voice. 'It's my name. Isobel Hutchings.'

'Jolly good,' I said.

'My question,' said Izzy Hutchings, 'is this. From where I sit and watch, there always seems to be so much going on at the church. How do you relax on a Sunday afternoon, between the morning services and the evening service?'

'Thank you for that question, Izzy,' I said. 'Well, Cheryl, of course, will answer for herself . . .' I could feel Cheryl's eyes on me saying, 'Don't be such a patronizing so-and-so.'

'But, as far as I'm concerned,' I continued, 'I spent last Sunday afternoon on women's deodorants.'

There was an embarrassed silence. I wasn't sure if this was because they all felt they hadn't heard me correctly, or because they believed that it was somehow not right and proper for a clergyman to spend his time in this way.

'I'm probably being a bit slow,' opined Colin, his voice rattling noticeably in his throat, 'but where do women's deodorants come in to this?'

'Where indeed!' I said heartily. 'Well, the fact is that we – that is, the advertising agency for which I work – were pitching for some new business with a deodorants company on Monday. And so I spent quite a lot of time on Sunday making sure I knew my stuff. On women's deodorants, that is.'

'How interesting,' mewed Mary Brown. I glanced at her fluttering eyelashes. How could anyone so immaculately made up and dressed so glamorously be called 'Brown'? 'And are these deodorants,' she continued, 'roll-ons or sprays?'

'Sprays,' I said. 'You probably know them, Mary. The

8

brand name is 'No Escape'. The name has a double meaning,' I continued, looking around at everyone else present. 'It refers both to the fact that no body odours will escape from you, and that', I coughed involuntarily, 'neither will the man you're after. Escape from you, I mean. If you wear it, that is.'

'Indeed!' snorted Doreen, confirmed in her suspicions that I was no more than a purveyor of all things salacious. Any comment she may have been about to make was, however, cut off by the strong but, by now, wobbly voice of John Burgess.

'Oh, woe!' he cried. 'Sprays! Who will pray for the ozone layer?'

I looked nervously across to Cheryl, who was biting her lip.

* * *

In the end, of course, Cheryl saved the day, somehow managing to say all the sorts of things that I wished I had been able to say. About trying to live the gospel in the world. About seeing what is sacred in those around us. About the need to set people free from whatever it is that weighs them down. And so on.

I could tell from the faces of all those present that they were captivated by Cheryl and what she had to say.

She then went on to talk about what it had meant to her to have me go forward to ordination. How she hoped she had supported me, but how it was not what she would have chosen. How it was something that God had thrown at her at just the time that everything else appeared to be falling into place. How, on the whole, she would rather see more of *me* and less of the church.

As usual I too became entranced by listening to her. I

was envious of the way she could speak so honestly about the church whilst, at the same time, conveying a simple and compelling faith. It was something that made us very different. I was always worrying about whether I was behaving, and feeling, like a Christian minister in the right way. Cheryl simply got on with it, patiently and faithfully.

'But that's enough of *my* views,' said Cheryl at last. 'Is there anything that anyone would like to say to me?'

'Yes,' said Izzy Hutchings, in her soft but imposing voice. 'You, Michael and Amy have been a clergy family for just six months. Did Michael's training prepare you for what life in the parish might be like after ordination?'

'Well, the first thing I have to say,' said Cheryl, 'is that Michael's training was just that. It was *Michael*'s training. There was no attempt to train me about anything. Which is probably just as well, because all this vocation stuff started just after Amy was born, so I had my hands pretty full. Don't get me wrong. I don't resent what Michael – what *we* – decided to do. But what that meant in practical terms was that I was left to be a single parent for much of the time while Michael went off to be holy and theological.'

Cheryl paused just long enough for me to feel embarrassed. For a few of those present it was probably the first time that they were aware that there had been a cost involved.

'To be honest,' continued Cheryl, 'having Michael as an ordained minister is a lot easier than having him in training. For one thing, I see a lot more of him. When he was training he'd be out most nights, and then rush off every fourth weekend for a residential course on something or other, leaving me at home to look after a small child single-handedly. I have to say, I almost think it would have been easier to deal with if he'd been having an affair!'

You could have heard a pin drop in Belinda Clubb's drawing room. A few eyes were turned towards me suspiciously as if I had, indeed, been having an affair.

'What do you mean by that exactly, Cheryl?' asked Doreen.

'Oh, just that at least *then* I would have known what he was doing!' quipped Cheryl with a broad smile across her face. The smile served to defuse the moment, and everyone felt permission to laugh.

'As it was . . .' she continued, but there was no need to end the sentence.

Yet again I was left feeling out of my depth. We had been invited as a couple to speak about 'The life of a new clergy family'. I had plunged in by talking about 'ministry' and my job. Cheryl had talked about service, and sacrifice, and truth, and love – in what she had felt, in how she had been, and in the way she had lived.

'Who would like some refreshment?' asked Belinda briskly. The general murmur of voices signalled that this would be a splendid idea. It was also the sign for any formality to dissipate into admiring conversations about the home-made cakes which were brought in only moments later to great acclaim.

'A wonderful addition to the Circle,' said Frank, looking at the cakes admiringly. 'Mrs Clubb, I mean. A woman who knows the way to a man's heart.'

Belinda Clubb looked suitably flattered and insisted that Frank was 'a one'. All of which helped contribute to the general air of good humour that, notwithstanding the thought of my 'affair', had descended on the gathering with the sharing of the tea and cake.

'You know,' said Cheryl, leaning across to whisper in

11

my ear, 'Jesus may have used bread and wine because they were there in the upper room, but I bet he would have used tea and cake if *that* had been the custom. After all, that's what everyone *here* will remember about *this* evening. Not your theology. Not my moaning. But Mrs Clubb's cakes. And, who knows, perhaps that's right.'

* * *

Over tea I chatted with Izzy Hutchings. Although I had seen her once or twice before, I knew nothing of her. She told me she was eighty-two years old and a former teacher of dance. She described her heyday as being 'coterminous with that of Clement Attlee', although she had not retired until Harold Wilson's first General Election win. With the conversation moving along these lines, it did not take me long to appreciate that Izzy was, and always had been, a member of the Labour Party – a leaning that made her a positive radical within the bounds of our very conservative parish.

'I bet you don't have too many parishioners who live quite so close to St Mary's as I do,' she said proudly.

'Why, where do you live?'

'Do you know Gracewell Court?'

'Right opposite the church?'

'Yes. Well, that's where I've lived for more than fifty years. And I don't think you can get nearer than that. You know, from my sitting room I can see through the vestry window.'

I was suddenly conscious of all the times over the last six months that I had dressed and undressed in that vestry.

'Do you know Josie, the nurse?' I asked, remembering the young woman I had met at the parish newcomers' party on Shrove Tuesday.

'Know her? She lives next door to me,' said Izzy. 'She said I can bang on the wall if I need her. Mind you, she's often not there, you know. She works very long shifts at the hospital.'

Finally, I couldn't resist asking the obvious question.

'Izzy, if you live so close to St Mary's, why don't you come more often?'

'Well, I *do* come, Michael,' she replied. 'That is, once in a while. I used to come a lot more. Years ago. But now not so much. Well, I'm getting old. And there are lots of people. And, well, *you* know.'

She smiled gently and looked towards the other folk in the room.

'I prefer a gathering like this,' she said. 'Not too many people. I don't like crowds, Michael. This is more my sort of thing. Yes, I know they're all a bit stuffy. Most of them still haven't forgiven Callaghan for devaluing the pound. But they're harmless enough. Doreen usually brings me. It's not always here, of course. First time I've been here. Doreen knew Belinda before. She only lives around the corner. So it's a bit out of her way to take me home. Still, she won't let me say no.'

I put a hand reassuringly on Izzy's arm.

'I'll take you back, Izzy. That is, Cheryl and I will. You're right on our way. We've got to go past St Mary's anyway.'

About twenty minutes later people started to make a move, and Cheryl and I prepared to leave with Izzy. As I headed for the door Frank Foster blocked my way, his eyes sparkling with his usual good humour.

'You know you were talking about deodorants,' he said. 'Well, I was thinking. Isn't "deo" Latin for "God"? Perhaps you could use that in your advertising. You know, something about a heavenly smell.'

13

I thanked Frank for his contribution, whilst Doreen looked on disdainfully. Frank, however, had not finished.

'Then you could come on wearing your dog collar and say "Let us spray".'

Frank grinned at his own joke. Doreen snorted, and I tried to slide past them to the door.

'You could even sell it to churches like St John's as incense in a can!' laughed Frank, clearly warming to his theme.

'Thank you, Frank,' I called back along the passage as I escaped out into the night air.

Cheryl and Izzy had been rather quicker in saying their goodbyes, and they were already waiting for me by the car. Ten minutes later the three of us arrived outside Izzy's door on the second floor of Gracewell Court. Izzy pointed out Josie's flat and told us once again about how she would bang on the wall if she needed help. She even showed us, hidden beneath a plant pot, the front-door key that she would use if she had left her key indoors. It was the same key that Josie would use if she needed to come in. It was clear that Izzy was proud of the relationship with her younger neighbour. Even though the two of them were, in their own ways, very independent women, I couldn't help thinking that they represented so much that was good about 'community'. Something we tried to create within the church, but also something that – with our differing personalities, needs and understandings – we seemed only to achieve on rare occasions. Regrettably, the evening with the Jubilee Circle did not feel like one of those occasions.

Cheryl and I walked back to the car to drive home and relieve the baby-sitter. My head was reeling with everything that had been said during the evening, but somehow Cheryl had managed to hang on to one particular comment that I had made as we first arrived at the meeting.

'You started saying something about bottles of Scotch,' she prompted me. 'What would I do if someone gave me three bottles of Scotch? What was that all about?'

The whisky. Of course. I had temporarily forgotten about the very thing that had been bothering me prior to the meeting at Mrs Clubb's.

'Oh, the Scotch', I replied with a sigh. 'Do you really want to hear about it?'

By way of reply Cheryl tipped her head on one side as if to say, 'When *don't* I want to hear?'

'Right,' I said, driving out of the car park at the back of Gracewell Court. 'Last week at the office I was sent three bottles of malt whisky. They came from Chris Mulligan. You remember? Frozen pizzas? Chris is the Marketing Manager of Pronto Pizzas. The bloke I spent some time with on Easter Saturday. It was a present. A thank you, I suppose.'

'Well, that's good, isn't it?' asked Cheryl.

'Yes, I suppose it is. But you see, I would have been pleased with just a thank you. Not three bottles of expensive Scotch. It didn't seem right. It *was* a personal matter after all. And I didn't feel comfortable having such a present delivered to the office. But then I realized that Chris wouldn't have known my home address. Just the phone number. Oh, I don't know. I guess I over-reacted.'

'Why? What did you do?'

'I sent the bottles back.'

I left a space for Cheryl to say something, but she was waiting for me to explain further.

'I sent them back,' I said again. 'I think I said

15

something about not being able to accept a gift that was so obviously expensive. That I didn't want any free spirits. That it might be seen to compromise my position. My ability to speak honestly or act in a personal capacity.'

'You actually said that?'

I looked across at Cheryl, and then turned the car into the road where we lived.

'You think I was wrong?' I asked sheepishly.

Cheryl inhaled deeply.

'Well,' she said, 'you could have just phoned the guy. Explained how you were feeling. Shared the drink around. Given it to charity. *I* don't know.'

There was just a hint of exasperation in her voice.

'Sorry,' she added. 'That doesn't help really, does it? So, tell me. What happened?'

I parked the car before continuing.

'Without knowing anything about the circumstances, Philip somehow got wind of the fact that I had returned a client gift.'

'Philip your boss?'

'Philip my boss. Yes. He called me in and told me I ought not to be so precious. That I shouldn't risk upsetting clients.'

We were still sitting in the car parked outside the house. There was a silence. Finally Cheryl asked, 'Did you explain to Philip that it was a personal matter and not a business matter?'

'No, I didn't,' I replied. 'I thought that would betray the confidence Chris Mulligan had placed in me.'

'But don't you think he betrayed *your* confidence by sending you the bottles?'

I was gripping the steering wheel tightly with my left hand. Cheryl took my hand in hers, unclenched it and smoothed it out gently.

16

'For what it's worth,' she said, 'I think you were right.'

'To send the spirits back?'

'Perhaps,' she said thoughtfully. 'I think you were right to do what you *felt* was right. But . . .'

'But what . . .?'

'Perhaps you should try less hard to be right.'

My face must have shown my confusion.

'Look,' said Cheryl. 'I'm not asking you to sacrifice your principles. Just relax a bit more, that's all. You've chosen a route that means you're going to get in a muddle every now and again. Whichever way you jump, you won't always win. You can never be the simple advertising man, any more than you can be the simple clergyman. And walking the border means there will always be some things that don't quite fit. You shouldn't take everything so seriously. That's what *I* think.'

'Perhaps,' I said. 'You're probably right.'

'Only probably?' said Cheryl. 'You don't sound convinced.'

'Well, I know it may sound silly,' I said, trying to find some kind of concluding comment, 'but I do have this feeling of mission. You talked earlier about setting people free. Well, I feel I have a mission to set people free in *some* way. I try to point people to God – at St Mary's, at St John's, the office, everywhere. But at the moment it just seems to be confusing me and everyone else as well. I suppose I'm just not comfortable with that.'

Cheryl squeezed my hand.

'Isn't that the point?' she said. 'Isn't that exactly the point about setting people free? You can't do it *for* them. You don't have to serve up neatly packaged little answers the whole time – either to them, or to yourself for that matter. The thing about faith is surely that it's bigger than any of us ever imagines. None of us really has a clue where throwing in our lot with God will take us. It's exciting. It's a bit dangerous even. Comfortable is the last thing it is. But isn't that also perhaps what makes the whole thing so, so worthwhile?'

I smiled back at her.

'You mean we're stuck with it,' I said. 'No escape, eh?'

'No escape?' Cheryl repeated, smiling. 'So we're back into women's deodorants now, are we?'

I looked at her blankly. Cheryl pulled a face.

'Women's deodorants,' she said again slowly. 'You can't have forgotten already! You were telling the Jubilee Circle about 'No Escape' and how it's supposed to make sure you get your man.'

'Oh, no!' I lamented, remembering the horrified looks on the faces of some of those present. 'Do you think they'll hold it against me?'

'Hold it against you?' said Cheryl. 'Well, all I can say is that when Mary Brown turns up for Communion on Sunday reeking of the stuff, you've only got yourself to blame!'

Be Prepared

Not one stone will be left here upon another;
all will be thrown down. Mark 13:2

ON the evidence of how much Mary's eyelashes were
fluttering on Sunday morning, Cheryl may well have
been right. I can't honestly say, however, that I
detected the familiar fragrance of 'No Escape' as I
helped distribute the bread and the wine during
the Communion. I was still at the point where taking
an active part in the service required my full and
undivided attention. It was very difficult to notice the
details of what people were wearing whilst trying to
manage a full chalice of wine.

The half-hour or so immediately after the service
was less fraught but more hectic, as I ricocheted from
one person to another in an attempt to talk to
everyone whom I had not managed to see in course of
the preceding week. Some of the conversations were
about setting up future meetings. Some were opportu-
nities for mutual pastoral support. Others were brief
exchanges on every subject from faith to photocopiers.

In addition, Sunday would not have been Sunday
without the usual range of helpful comments from the
more familiar members of the flock: Doreen informing
me that I had read the gospel too quickly or too slowly,
too loudly or too quietly; Barbara suggesting that I
should have more sensitivity than to wear suede shoes
with my cassock; John Burgess declaring vehemently,
after one of my sermons, that 'Judgment awaits!'; Joy,

who was famous for her *non sequiturs*, sharing with me the view, when I asked for volunteers to help with the jumble sale, that 'Going metric will only make matters worse'.

So it was that, as Pentecost approached, I began to think of ways in which I might find some space, of ways in which I might find room for the Holy Spirit in what was becoming a very busy schedule. Finding time on my own was, of course, not usually easy: quite naturally I enjoyed spending as much of my weekends as possible with Cheryl and Amy. When one Saturday morning, however, they were both out with friends at the same time, I took the opportunity to visit St Mary's in search of inspiration.

As I entered the church building I experienced an immediate feeling of peace. The place appeared to be completely empty. Not a sound could be heard except the noise of my heels on the flagstones. Sunlight was cascading in through the south windows. I walked to the back of the church and sat down in the rearmost pew staring forward, my eyes scanning the size and glory of the vaulted interior.

On most occasions when I was in the church there was always so much going on, so many people about, that I was never able to absorb the wonder and scale of the place, the resonance in the air, the sense of presence, the history. And also the timeless space for meeting God. In the shafts of light that angled their way through the glass and on to the stone it was easy to imagine a world of bright angelic spirits moving between and through the sometimes heavy structure of the church.

I closed my eyes and breathed deeply for a few moments, before releasing my thoughts into prayer.

Great God, Heavenly Father,
Fill me with your light.
Please.
Move in me, and lift my spirit.
Please.
And help me, in this place,
To help others touch something
Of your wonder and grace.
Thank you.

I opened my eyes, roused myself from my reverie and
began to make my way slowly along the nave towards
the altar, feeling the end of each pew as I went. I imagined the rows full of people, all eager for the coming of
Pentecost: faces lit up with expectation, minds willing
the Holy Spirit to move them, hearts eager to change
and grow.

But this, I reflected, was not the congregation of St
Mary's and St John's. One day, perhaps, but not now.

It was then I saw something hit the floor a few feet
ahead of me. Something that had fallen from somewhere above. Something small bouncing on the flagstones before coming to rest by the side of one of the
pews. I moved towards it and picked it up. It appeared
to be a small piece of stone, uneven and no more than
a couple of centimetres in width. Close by were several
more pieces covering an area a few feet across. I
stepped back towards the place from where the first
piece appeared to have fallen and looked up. I could
see nothing except the top of a wide pillar where it
sprouted proudly into the arches which supported the
main span of the church roof.

And then it hit me, another small piece of stone, or
plaster, or whatever it might have been. I felt it on my
head like a drop of rain, and then it too tumbled to the

ground and bounced harmlessly to one side. I stooped and picked it up, knowing only that it was a piece of the fabric of the church. For a second I imagined the whole roof collapsing about my ears, and then the true irony of the moment hit me.

Here was I, thinking of the Holy Spirit, daring to hope that the church might be filled with the light and power of such an inspiration. And then, in the midst of my dreaming, a tiny piece of masonry falls upon me, reminding me that *this* church is also a construction made by human hands, a pile of stone and mortar. And, what's more, one which looked as if it was about to start falling down.

There was obviously only one thing to do. I left the church immediately to find the vicar, Canon George Finney.

* * *

On my way to the vicarage I bumped into Frank Foster, the St Mary's churchwarden, and the person most concerned with the day-to-day upkeep of the church building.

'Ah, just the chap,' I said, greeting him.

Frank grinned at me, his ruddy face a picture of practicality.

'That must mean trouble,' said Frank. 'So what have you broken?'

I pulled a face and told him he must be thinking of someone else.

'Probably some other curate,' grinned Frank. 'You're all the same. Stipendiary or non-stipendiary. In my experience, curates break things. That chap we had four years ago – Julian ·· he broke loads of things. So what's broken? You didn't touch the sanctuary rail, did you?'

'Sanctuary rail? No. Why?'

'Well, because it's just been repaired, that's why. And beautifully too. Some of that wood was rotten right through and I thought we'd never find someone who could do some invisible mending on it. But I was lucky enough to be put in touch with a skilled carpenter who lives right here in the parish. Right under our noses. And he did a beautiful job on it. You'd hardly know it was new wood.'

'Well, you can breathe easy,' I said, 'I haven't even touched the sanctuary rail. But I think I may have broken the church itself.'

'You've broken the church?' said Frank, the grin suddenly disappearing from his face.

'It may not have been me, of course,' I replied. It was now my turn to smile. 'But it looks all up for St Mary's for the time being.'

This last remark was clearly made in jest. If I had known, however, how prophetic it was to be, I dare say that I would not have said it.

Frank was now in serious mode and without further ado he ushered me into the vicarage where the vicar of St Mary's and St John's was waiting for him.

'So,' said Canon George, his round, plump, calm face exuding peace and good sense. 'Let's start at the beginning, shall we?'

The three of us were now sitting with mugs of coffee in Canon George's study.

'Shall we start with what you seem to have discovered?' he said, looking at me in that understanding way that seemed untouched by the minor troubles of this world.

I responded by re-telling exactly what had happened from the moment I stepped through the church door some half-hour before, right up to my meeting with Frank in front of the vicarage.

'To be honest,' said Frank, 'it doesn't surprise me. The report of the diocesan surveyor pointed to subsidence and indicated that the whole church was going downhill.'

I breathed a sigh of relief that John and Rose Burgess were not there to hear this being said.

'I think, to be fair,' said Canon George, smiling broadly, 'the diocesan surveyor's comments were about St Mary's and not the Church of England as a whole. And, anyway, I thought you said that he had purposely been, how shall I say, "overly cautious" in his diagnosis. Wasn't that the gist of your discussion with him a few weeks ago?'

'"Overly cautious" sums him up very well,' said Frank, coughing and beginning to become animated on the subject. 'I think his parents should have called him Prudence. If he worked for an insurance company he would never give anyone life cover on the basis that, in the end, we all die.'

I laughed, although I wasn't sure that Frank had meant to make a joke of it.

'Well, exactly,' said Canon George. 'So I thought you and he had agreed that there was no immediate urgency in the matter. He as good as told you, didn't he Frank, that he felt he couldn't be too careful? He didn't want another St Helena's after all.'

'St Helena's?' I said. 'The church that was wrecked during the great storm of '87?'

'The very one,' said Canon George. 'The diocesan surveyor had given St Helena's his blessing, as it were, only weeks before. And then the wind blew down the steeple which crashed through the roof of the church. Fortunately it was the dead of night and no one was hurt. Even so. Once bitten, as they say.'

'Oh, I see,' I said. But I wasn't sure that I did. Did that

mean that St Mary's *was*, or was *not*, going down the hill?

'Basically, we thought that things were not as bad as was first feared,' said Frank, seeing my puzzled look. 'But your experience in the church just now suggests that it was our optimism that was the problem rather than the diocesan surveyor's innate caution.'

'Well, whatever the case, one way or another,' said Canon George, 'we clearly need to alert the arch-deacon as soon as possible – and presumably get someone from the surveyor's office back again. And in the meantime . . .'

'Yes,' said Frank, feeling the need for action and reaching for a pen in order to make a list.

'. . . in the meantime,' continued the vicar, 'I think we do two things. We close the church for anything other than supervised visits. And we pray.'

* * *

That evening I had agreed to spend some time with the scouts who met in St Mary's church hall. The scout troop was not officially linked to St Mary's and St John's, although there had been occasions when it had been involved in special services and fund-raising events. Over the years, therefore, a certain affinity had grown up between the scouts and the parish. As far as I could make out, the scouts never came to church of their own free will, and so having them in the church hall once a week was at least a way of building some kind of relationship with the boys – and now, of course, girls as well.

The scouts were kept in order by two leaders, Jack and Don. Jack was a somewhat wizened and weather-beaten man who had been talking about his approach-ing retirement for as long as anyone could remember.

He had to be seventy years old if he was a day, but was always very keen to give the impression that he was no more than forty. It was the sort of spirit I really admired, and I marvelled at the amount of energy he showed week after week in dealing with a fairly boisterous group of boys and girls between the ages of eleven and fourteen.

Don was quite a contrast. A barrel-chested and moustachioed Liverpudlian, no more than half Jack's age, Don was a taciturn but kindly figure of authority who commanded immediate respect from even the most cocksure of children. I had first met Don the year before when the scouts had run a stall at the parish summer fayre, and had immediately taken to his blunt and no-nonsense approach to everything, and everyone, around him.

Jack and Don were both nominally Christian, occasionally turning up to special services, and they always finished the scout meetings with a prayer. They were conscious, however, that the troop still remained largely outside the sphere of influence of the church and that perhaps more could be done to interest the scouts in parish activities. It was for this reason that they had invited me along to one of their sessions to meet the scouts and to show them around St Mary's.

'Were *you* ever a scout?' asked one lad boldly after I was introduced to them by Jack. We were sitting around informally in the church hall, although I had come straight from work and so looked slightly incongruous in my linen suit and loud silk tie. My questioner must have been about thirteen years old, with a shock of copper-coloured hair and a haze of freckles across his open face. He obviously felt it was his business to move things along and get some kind of conversation going with this strange-looking person

26

who claimed to be a clergyman but was clearly nothing of the sort.

'Yes,' I answered truthfully. 'Yes, I was.'

'Why?' came a small gruff voice from somewhere below me. I looked down to see a younger round-faced, fair-haired boy with glasses, contorting his face into a picture of unnatural inquisitiveness.

'Why?' I repeated. 'Well, er,' I stammered, not knowing the young inquisitor's name.

'Edwin,' the inquisitor volunteered.

I looked back at him suspiciously, convinced that his name was probably nothing of the sort, but without the conviction to confront him on the matter.

'Well, er, Edwin,' I said. 'I was a scout because it gave me an opportunity to do all sorts of things that I wasn't able to do at school.'

As I said it I knew that this was the sort of answer likely to be misunderstood.

'Like what?'

It was the red-headed lad again, who, as I found out later, went by the name of Adam. It was a simple and obvious question, but my mind suddenly went blank. I could think of nothing other than camping and tying knots.

'Well,' I said hesitantly. 'Camping and tying knots, to name just two.'

'What did you like about tying knots?' said Edwin's neighbour, a plump girl who looked as if she might have had some Amazon blood in her. I stared at her dumbly, beginning to think that my afternoon presenting the agency's new creative strategy for Macro Suds Washing Liquid had been a doddle compared to this.

'What did I like about tying knots?' I mused aloud. 'Well, I suppose it was a perfect training for my current role in the parish. After all, I'm always getting myself tied up in knots!'

Not a glimmer. Not a hint in the faces of the assembled scouts that this comment might have been even just a teeny-weeny bit funny. Instead, they all stared back at me with implacable faces. Cut the waffle, the faces seemed to say. Just answer the question.

'They're not backward in coming forward,' said Don, when we stopped mid-session for a cup of tea.

'They're quite an intrepid lot, really,' added Jack. 'Which is probably just as well these days.'

'Intrepid's the word,' I said. 'I'd rather have them *for* me than against me.'

Jack laughed. Don bit thoughtfully into a biscuit.

'I bet you're thinking particularly of the Browning boys,' said Jack. 'Adam and Edwin. Fearless they are. Mind you,' he said, dropping his voice, 'they've had to look after themselves quite a lot. Their parents,' he said, winking at me in a very pointed manner.

I craned forward, unsure as to what he was trying to communicate.

'Nutty as fruitcakes,' added Don flatly. 'Father's a painter, mother's an actress. Barking mad, they are.'

I must have looked unsure of Don's use of language, for he felt the need to reiterate.

'Barking mad,' he said again.

'Really,' I said at last, hoping that my expression conveyed an appropriate amount of sympathy and understanding.

'And that, er, well-built young lady who was sitting next to Edwin,' I continued. 'She also seemed quite outspoken.'

'Gemma,' said Jack. 'Gemma Dooley. She's fourteen and something of a big sister to all the boys. I hear that she also packs quite a punch. You know what I mean.

She can flatten any boy that gets out of line.'

I nodded. From what I was hearing, this was definitely a group of scouts that I would want to have on my side.

As I carried on chatting with Jack, Don called the twenty or so scouts to order for what was to be the second half of the evening. A guided tour of the inside of the church, with yours truly commenting on the historical and architectural points of interest.

We walked together along the path to St Mary's and I opened the west door so that everyone could pass straight through to the back of the church, from where I proposed to start the tour. I asked the group to wait there while I went to put on the lights, for the sunlight was now beginning to fade and the building was brimming with shadows. Had the scouts appeared less self-assured I might have made some comment about it all looking 'a bit spooky'. This lot, however, did not seem likely to be worried by a few dark corners.

By the time I came back the building was bathed in light. I made a brief explanation of the fact that, for the time being, entry to the church could only be under supervision, and then embarked on the guided tour.

As I moved around the church I had the distinct impression that the scouts were only staying close to me because Jack and Don were bringing up the rear. I noticed several sidelong glances that suggested that some kind of game played in and out of the pews would be infinitely preferable to anything this vicar bloke might choose to say.

I nevertheless stuck to my task and led the scouts around the building, stopping every now and again to point out something that I thought might interest them.

'This is the font,' I said. 'This is where new Christians are baptized.'

'What about *old* Christians?' came a gruff voice. Edwin was looking at me with the kind of intensity that I found rather menacing. 'Where are *they* baptized?'

'*Old* Christians,' I mused aloud. 'Well, er, Edwin. All old Christians were new Christians once upon a time.'

Edwin appeared unconvinced by this response.

'In the bath,' added Adam helpfully. 'They do old Christians in a bath. They stick their heads under.'

Edwin was now nodding. His brother's answer was clearly more helpful than mine.

'This is more of a sink,' continued Adam, indicating the font. 'If you don't fit in the sink, they put you in the bath.'

I tried to make eye contact with the two brothers, but failed. Were they having me on?

'Let's move on, shall we?' I said at last, shepherding them towards the pulpit. The main point of interest with the pulpit concerned how many scouts could fit inside it. Having managed to squeeze twelve of themselves into it, they were of the opinion that pulpits were a good idea and that there should be a lot more of them.

'Look at this,' called Gemma to the boys as they clattered down the steps of the pulpit. She was pointing to a stone set into the wall of the north aisle.

'It says here that "one Jofias Falter paffed away in 1628". What does that mean?'

Adam was immediately to the fore once more.

'They used a twenty-four hour clock in those days. 1628 means nearly half past four.'

Again I looked at him suspiciously.

'Not that, you twit!' continued Gemma. 'Paffed. What's paffed? It says he paffed away. What's paffing?'

I suppressed a chuckle.

'It means "passed away",' I said. 'In other words, he died. They used to write their "Ss" like "Fs" in those days. What it says is "one Josias Salter passed away in 1628".'

Gemma and several of the other scouts nodded seriously. Edwin and Adam turned to each other with mischievous grins on their faces. Oh dear, I thought, I can already imagine what *they'll* spend the rest of the evening thinking about: how to turn 'S' words into 'F' words!

It was with the intention of getting their minds on to something more educational that I started outlining the history of the church. I moved away from Josias Salter and pointed out several of the other inscriptions around the place, mentioning what had been happening in the world at various key dates: 1665, 1815, 1914.

While I was doing this I kept an eye on the faces of Adam, Edwin and Gemma. I had already decided that these three would provide the best indication of the interest level among the scouts.

Not surprisingly, perhaps, it soon became clear that their interest level was at its highest whenever I mentioned some historical figure who had died horribly, or a war, or some other major catastrophe. A particular 'hit' was the Great Plague. In this respect, I could see that their overriding view was that the church was no more than a gigantic tomb – and a place more about death than life.

This worried me, and so I tried to turn my guided tour into something of a description of present-day life in the church. Having pointed out the various physical features, and outlined something of the history, I then briefly referred to the sorts of things that went on inside the building. Marriages, blessings, meetings, music, teaching, services – worship in all its many forms.

The faces around me, however, began to look bored. Whereas things like the 'sink', and the idea of 'paffing' had just about kept their attention, the notion of 'worship' seemed to be somehow more of an embarrassment than anything else. Oh well, I thought, perhaps now was not the time to try to push water uphill.

With these thoughts in my mind, I led the group back along the nave and past the place where earlier that day the small piece of masonry had fallen on my head. Canon George had agreed that I could take the scouts around the building as planned, but that the church should remain locked until such time as the surveyor had made his pronouncements.

It was therefore with some nervousness that I looked up and then down at the flagstones beneath my feet. There appeared to be no further signs of impending collapse and so we passed on through the church and returned to the west end from where we had started our tour.

'You'll notice,' I said, looking around at the blank expressions, 'that this part of the church, where we are standing now, looks a lot newer than the rest. That's because a bomb dropped by a German warplane in 1940 fell just outside and destroyed the original west-end porch and part of the west-end wall.'

At a stroke I had regained their full and undivided attention. A bomb. A war. Something destroyed. Now we were *really* talking!

Feeling that I had at least concluded the visit with something of a triumph, I turned to lead the group back out through the door. It was then that Jack spoke.

'Aren't you going to mention the ghost, Michael?' he said.

Ghost? Who said ghost?

Around me the scouts had stopped in their tracks. A ghost! Here in the local church! A ring of faces stared in my direction, waiting for what I would say next. The only problem was that I knew nothing at all about any ghost story. Jack's words had taken me by surprise as much as anyone. Rather than show my ignorance immediately, however, I decided to bluff.

'Well, why don't you do the ghost bit, Jack?'

Which he did. There was talk, so it was said, that a tramp had been sleeping rough around St Mary's at the time the bomb had fallen in October 1940. Whatever the scouts may have thought about this, my own mind was suddenly filled with an image of Josh MacDonald and the incident that had dominated the Easter just past.

As regards the tramp of 1940, it was said that his favourite sleeping place was the west-end porch – a place that offered shelter from the chill wind. No human remains had been found among the rubble after the blast, and so there was no real reason to believe that the tramp had been a victim of the bomb. Nevertheless, parishioners declared that he was never seen again after the bomb went off. All of which prompted the notion that he had been blown into oblivion on that fateful night and that his ghost still walked the church on the anniversary of his death – the eve of All Hallows.

Jack told the story with relish and missed no opportunity to add what I guessed must have been details of his own fabrication. The scouts were clearly entranced by the tale, however, and immediately wanted to know if I had seen the ghost, and if they could see it too. So much for getting them interested in the church – everything I had said was already forgotten!

I fended off the questions, largely by insisting on the fact that I had not had the pleasure of seeing the ghost, and that I honestly knew no one who had. As my declaration appeared to be viewed with distrust by most of the young people present, however, I was very grateful when Jack and Don took charge by marshalling the scouts and leading them back to the church hall for the final minutes of their meeting.

'Where on earth did you get that ghost story from?' I asked Jack when all the scouts had finally gone home. 'I'll admit now that I've not heard anything like it before.'

Jack laughed, and I wondered if he had made it up there and then.

'It wouldn't surprise me if the vicar hadn't heard it either,' he said. 'The fact is, my father told me. He was a regular here at St Mary's during the war. And *he* got the story off the verger who was here then. Not the one before Colin, but the one before that. Wilfred, I think his name was.'

I smiled and reflected on what Jack had said. How could a story with so little substance have gained such a hold and still, fifty years later, instantly captivate the otherwise impenetrable minds of the St Mary's scouts? And why, when I had tried to convey the *real* spiritual life of the church, had they found it all so boring?

I made a mental note to talk to Canon George on the subject at some time, and then I left Jack and Don to clear away. Leaving the hall I wandered back up the path and along the side of the church building which was now silhouetted against a blue-black sky. Tomorrow the diocesan surveyor was due to make an urgent visit following a phone call from Canon George that made it clear that the situation might be something of an emergency.

Once again an assessment would be made of the pile of stone and history that I had endeavoured to bring to life for the scouts, the pile of stone and history that had come most alive for them through Jack's telling of the ghost story. I tried not to feel too gloomy. If *that* ghost could capture their interest and imagination, then why not the Holy Ghost? The potential seemed to be there for some kind of dialogue with the scouts. A dialogue that might go so much further than any dry description of a past fossilized in stone. A dialogue that might reach out to touch something of spirit and something of the future. The kind of future for which these young people might not otherwise be prepared.

But how? That was the question that was in my mind as I made my way home that night. How could I, or anyone else, turn those inquisitive and robust minds into real free spirits? Free spirits with a sense of God as something – someone – bigger than this building, and bigger than anything that went on inside it.

What I should have been worried about, in retrospect, was what was going on in the scouts' minds as they made *their* way home. The ghost story was going to haunt us for quite some time.

THREE

Make Ready

*'All these things my hand has made, and so all
these things are mine.'* Isaiah 66:2

THE joint Parochial Church Council, the PCC, of St
Mary's and St John's met during the week following
the survey of St Mary's. It was the middle of May, and
the evenings were now light and even quite warm. As I
made my way from the railway station to St Mary's
church hall, I passed several people dressed in summer
clothes who were clearly enjoying the first taste of a
new season. A blackbird was singing its heart out from
a rooftop that glowed deep red in the late sun. With
that song resonating in my soul, I was determined to be
positive about the news of St Mary's – whatever it
might be.

That news would as yet be known only to Canon
George. This emergency meeting of the PCC had been
convened at short notice on the basis of the surveyor's
promise to provide the vicar with a verbal report this
very afternoon. The full written report would follow in
the days ahead, but Canon George had been very keen
that the PCC should have the very earliest opportunity
to hear the news as a corporate body.

As I walked past the church, Colin was just letting
himself out of a side door. Colin represented the
Catholic leaning within the worshipping community
of St Mary's. In many ways he would have been
happier with the style of worship at the parish's
daughter church, St John's. Stephen Pickle, the priest-

in-charge there, practised a slightly 'higher' tradition than was appropriate for St Mary's – although it still stopped short of being always 'smells and bells'.

Quite apart from his own personal taste, however, Colin felt a great sense of loyalty to St Mary's. Perhaps it was more a sense of ownership. But *whatever* it was, it had found its expression in the twenty years of time and energy that he had invested in the church at the top of the hill.

He looked across at the pale grey suit and red polo shirt that he saw coming towards him, and his long face creased into a smile as soon as he made out who it was. He called out 'Good evening, Father', and waved his arm, making an indistinct salute in my direction. I joined him on the path that led down through the churchyard to the car park and the hall, and there we bumped into Lynda Soames.

Lynda was the most prominent of the evangelical set amongst our largely middle-of-the-road congregation, and was therefore something of a counter-balance to Colin. Despite that – or perhaps *because* of it – there always seemed to be a certain affinity between them.

'Good evening, Lynda,' croaked Colin in his most affectionate manner.

'Hello, verger,' said Lynda. 'And hello, Michael. How's Cheryl?'

I don't think Lynda ever asked me how *I* was. She always asked about Cheryl. I suppose it was very caring really, but there was still a bit of me that always wanted to say pointedly, 'Cheryl's fine – but I'm actually not so good myself.'

'Cheryl's fine,' I said, smiling and adding nothing more than a confirmatory nod.

'And Amy?'

'She's fine too,' I said.

'And how old is she now?' asked Lynda.

'Thirty-three, I think.'

Lynda huffed. She didn't like my so-called sense of humour.

'Amy – not Cheryl,' she said flatly.

'Five,' I said. 'Yes, she's still only five. Although you wouldn't believe it sometimes.' I sighed, before adding, 'And how is . . .?'

I couldn't for the life of me think of the name of Lynda's husband, whom I had not met.

'Gordon?' she suggested.

I assumed Gordon to be the husband in question, and stuck boldly to my task.

'And how is Gordon?' I asked.

Lynda looked up at me meaningfully, her large eyes glowing in a way that I found a bit threatening.

'I'm still praying for him,' she said.

'Oh, right, right,' I stammered, not sure what all this was about. 'Jolly good,' I said, nodding enthusiastically at Lynda's obvious perseverance. Feeling, however, that my positive response might not necessarily be interpreted in the right spirit, I added quickly and slightly insensitively, 'What's he got then?'

Lynda cast her large eyes heavenward. Oh, dear, I thought.

'It's not what he's got,' she said at last. 'It's what he *hasn't* got.'

Feeling by now way out of my depth, but also aware that there was really nothing for it but to press on, I said warily,

'So what *hasn't* he got then?'

'The Holy Spirit,' she said slowly and ominously.

'Oh, is *that* all,' I started to say with an air of naked relief. Seeing, however, a horrified look forming on her face, I quickly mutated the 'all' into something approaching the 'awful'. All of which meant that my final strangulated sentence came out as something like, 'Oh, is *that* allllwwful thing still happening?'

The emerging look of horror on Lynda's face transformed itself into a picture of total incomprehension. She was not able to articulate any feelings she may have had at that moment, however, for our rather inauspicious conversation was interrupted by Geoffrey Newton as we neared the door of the hall.

'Hello, brothers and sister,' crowed Geoffrey, waving a book in our direction. I could almost feel a tightening in the bodies of Colin and Lynda. Geoffrey was our Don Cupitt-in-residence who loved nothing better than theological controversy. The more outlandish the views, the better, as far as he was concerned.

'Have you read this?' he asked. 'It's terribly good.'

'And what might that be?' asked Colin politely, fumbling in his pocket for his spectacles.

'It's called *How Man Created God*. Frightfully good read.'

'Don't you mean *How God Created Man*?' asked Colin, somewhat innocently.

Geoffrey laughed. Lynda coughed. I tried to look as if it were all nothing to do with me. I couldn't cope with one of Geoffrey's vigorous debates just before a PCC meeting.

Geoffrey and his wife Amanda were both in their mid-thirties, and always likely to have read the latest liberal analysis of the religious state of mind. Geoffrey stood there rocking backwards and forwards in his scuffed Dr Marten shoes and baggy corduroys. With his bright, smiling eyes and ready smile, you couldn't help but like him.

'That's the whole point, Colin,' he continued, handing the verger the book. *How Man Created God*, you see.

It's about the way in which man has created God in his own image. You know the sort of thing. To fulfil all man's spiritual needs.'

'And where does *woman* fit into all this?'

This sharp interpolation came from Penny Wainwright – the tall and rather assertive leader of the St Mary's Sunday School. Colin, meanwhile, was still opening and closing his mouth, utterly lost for words, and holding the book as if it were red-hot coals.

'Let's go in,' I said hastily, shepherding Colin, Lynda, Geoffrey and Penny into the hall. It was at times like this that I really began to understand the role of the pastor as shepherd, trying somehow to hold together the disparate views and personalities that exist in any local church. To be honest, I was rather glad that the parish of St Mary's and St John's had so many diverse views within it. I couldn't help thinking that our faith was more likely to be kept alive by such a diversity of views than it was by grey uniformity. Not that such diversity always made for an easy life. It certainly wasn't going to tonight.

As we entered the hall I could see that most of the members of the PCC were already there. The PCC was, in some ways I suppose, an approximation of 'the mind of the parish church community'. PCC meetings were times when I would see together in one place the active parishioners from St John's as well as those from St Mary's. People like Hilary Noble, a daunting female solicitor and our honorary parish secretary, or Alan Watts, the churchwarden of St John's, a retired civil servant and a disturbingly efficient administrator.

A PCC meeting could often be the occasion for long and convoluted discussion on almost any subject related to local church affairs. On this particular evening, however, there could be only one subject of conversation and one main speaker – the vicar.

There was a hushed silence as Canon George brought the meeting to order and stared benevolently around at the twenty or so assembled faces. He opened proceedings with a prayer, and then began his report on the pressing matter of the St Mary's survey. As he was beginning, Stephen Pickle slipped in and sat down next to me.

'Well,' began the vicar, 'as I've heard said in this hall on another occasion like this, there's some good news and there's some bad news. Let me start with the good news. The good news is that the surveyor has given St Mary's a thorough going-over, and the problem really isn't as bad as we first thought.'

Canon George paused to allow time for this piece of communication to sink in. It was long enough to provoke a response from certain quarters.

'May I interrupt?' asked Alan Watts in a very grave tone. 'Do you mean it's not as bad as we first thought in the first place, or not as bad as we thought after we'd realized that it wasn't as bad as we first thought?'

Canon George stared back at Alan, an initial smile slowly draining from his face.

'I'm not sure I quite follow,' said the vicar.

'If I may interpolate,' said Hilary, sitting bolt upright and straightening the skirt of her smart suit. 'I surmise that the churchwarden for St John's is referring, some-what obliquely, to the following chain of events. In September of last year there occurred, at St Mary's, the regrettable incident of the slates falling from the roof and damaging several of the headstones in the churchyard. Pursuant to that incident, recorded in the minutes of the PCC of 28th September, this body requested that the diocesan surveyor review the church structure. His initial report was presented to the PCC in January of this year, and Section III 4 (b) ii outlined a situation which suggested that there was a possibility of some subsidence.'

'Oh, of course,' whispered Stephen Pickle sarcastically in my ear. 'Who could forget Section III 4 (b) ii? It was a stonking read, as far as I can remember. Not as good as Section VIII 2 (q) xxvi, but pretty close.'

Hilary glowered over the top of her half-moon spectacles at the interruption, and then carried on.

'This, I believe, was the very *first* first that Alan was talking about, Mr Chairman. That meeting in January, however, requested that the churchwarden of St Mary's should undertake further discussions with the diocesan surveyor in order to establish the magnitude of the problem.'

I could see Frank Foster's ruddy face nodding seriously in agreement.

'Those discussions, Mr Chairman,' continued Hilary, 'indicated that the problem was not as bad as we had heretofore assumed, and no further action was deemed necessary. Then, two weeks ago, the Reverend Michael Dunn noticed the presence of some debris in the church that seemed to indicate a related problem. This gave rise to the assumption that any earlier sense of relief was in fact unfounded, and that the original bad news was indeed just that. Bad news. This was the *second* of the firsts to which the churchwarden of St John's was referring.'

Alan Watts nodded, although it was not clear whether this was through agreement or sleep.

'It was that second incident that led to the return of the surveyor last week for a further inspection of the structure – a verbal report of which was transmitted to the vicar this afternoon. Is that clear?'

'Very clear,' fibbed Canon George. I thought no one

else would dare intervene, but I was wrong. Doreen Butcher was not the sort of lady to be implicated in any corporate misunderstanding.

'Let me get this straight,' she said. 'We thought St Mary's was falling down. Then we thought it wasn't falling down. Then we thought it was falling down again. And that's why the surveyor came back.'

'You've got it, Doreen!' said Frank admiringly.

'So what did the surveyor say *this* time?' came an imperious voice from the back. It was the voice of Barbara Bailey, the tall and imposing sacristan of St Mary's, and a woman who was held by common opinion to resemble assorted senior members of the royal family. 'Are we up or are we down?' asked Barbara sternly.

'Well, if you'll all bear with me,' said Canon George, showing his usual and remarkable patience, 'I'm just coming to that.' He smiled that special smile of his, and immediately the frustration that had been brewing amongst the gathered church worthies melted away. An atmosphere of tolerance and understanding once more settled on the meeting as Canon George continued his report.

'So the good news is that things are not as bad as were first feared – and *that*, Alan, covers not only our fears in January, but also our fears last week. The surveyor's view is that it's not subsidence, after all. The church is, in fact, in a settled position : . .'

'*Too* settled, if you ask me,' whispered Stephen.

'. . . but there *has* been some movement over time, and this has caused a loosening of some of the stonework high up on the pillars. This is not, in itself, a matter of urgency, in so far as the church is not going to collapse . . .'

'Don't you believe it,' whispered Stephen.

'. . . but it *is* urgent in so far as we clearly cannot continue to worship in St Mary's until some kind of remedial work has been carried out. The alternative would be to risk injury from small pieces of falling stone.'

There was silence in the hall. Even Stephen was now respectfully quiet.

'I'm still waiting, of course, for the full details of what this will entail. But the indications from the surveyor are that St Mary's will have to be closed for worship for a significant period whilst scaffolding is erected inside the church and the necessary work completed. It could be three months, it could be longer. I shall be asking Colin to maintain some kind of oversight of the building during this time. The church will be opened for necessary and supervised maintenance. For the rest of the time, however, I am very much afraid that St Mary's will be temporarily closed.'

Looking around and seeing the glum faces of those PCC members who were stalwarts of the St Mary's congregation, Canon George added,

'Remember – we're very lucky, really.'

The notion of being 'very lucky' seemed to have escaped everyone.

'We're very lucky,' continued the vicar, 'because we have two churches in the parish. And while the church at the top of the hill is closed, those of us who are more used to worshipping at St Mary's can enjoy a bit of a break by going down the hill to St John's.'

We were supposed to be one united parish, sharing two churches and one vicar. Even so, the lack of enthusiasm for this idea from all concerned was only too evident. One parish we might be, but everyone had his or her especial affiliation to one or other of the churches. Canon George did not, however, want to lose the chance to sound a note of unity in the face of adversity.

'Yes,' he said in as chirpy a tone as he could muster. 'It will be good for all of us. A united parish, united in prayer at one church for the work that has to be done at the other.'

There was a taut silence, at the end of which several people chipped in with their comments.

'Well, just so long as I don't have to do any of that bowing and scraping,' said Lynda.

'Genuflection is purely optional,' added Hilary helpfully.

'I had a friend called Jen,' mused Joy loudly. 'But she went to live in Scunthorpe.'

'Will there be incense?' asked Penny. 'Only I'm not sure it's good for the children.'

'I'm not coming if there's smoke,' said Doreen sternly. 'It plays havoc with my sinuses. I knew a man who died once.'

'Of incense?' said Alan. 'What was he doing with it, for goodness sake?'

Doreen looked aggrieved by Alan's suggestion that the person referred to was in some way implicated in substance abuse.

'I knew a man who died,' said Joy. 'He's dead now though.'

Just as the hubbub of conversation seemed to be verging on the absurd, Frank's voice brought everyone back to the main matter in hand.

'You said, vicar, that St Mary's could be closed for three months, but that it could be longer. How *much* longer?'

Canon George pulled thoughtfully on his chin before replying.

'Well, there's the rub, you see, Frank. Before the

diocese can sanction the work to start, the parish has to make a commitment to come up with a large proportion of the necessary funds. If the work begins straightaway, then it should be done in about three months. If the decision is delayed, then it will take longer.'

'Then we have to make that commitment,' said Doreen in her best Churchillian manner. 'We *have* to make that commitment.'

'I agree with Doreen,' intoned Barbara Bailey. 'We cannot stand by and see St Mary's closed for more time than is absolutely necessary. We *must* commit ourselves to finding the money.'

There was a general chorus of approval from the members of the St Mary's congregation. It was clearly an emotional response rather than a rational response – we had received, after all, no firm indication of how much all this would cost. That cost was likely to be considerable, I assumed. Certainly thousands of pounds. Perhaps tens of thousands. But then, faced with that kind of challenge, perhaps an emotional response was precisely what was needed.

Canon George stilled the continuing murmurs with the slightest wave of his hand.

'I have to say I'm inclined to agree,' he said. 'I believe we must, somehow, make that commitment. But that has two very important implications. First, we must make sure that we leave no stone unturned in terms of fund-raising activities between now and the end of the year.'

He paused, long enough for the penny to drop. Long enough for the message to sink in.

'And the second implication?' prompted Frank, although I could see from the look in his eyes that, on *this* occasion, he already knew what the vicar would say.

'The second thing,' said Canon George, 'is that we must pray. We must pray for all the help the Lord can give us in overcoming this little local difficulty.'

The rest of the meeting was given over to the subject of money and the sorts of events that could be undertaken in the way of fund-raising. The money raised by the Summer Fayre, already planned for next month, would be channelled in this direction. The various church groups in the parish would be asked to organize their own fund-raising events. It was also suggested that those non-church organizations that used the hall on a regular basis be invited to consider ways in which they might be able to help. I immediately thought of the scouts, and wondered what the likes of Adam, Edwin and Gemma might suggest.

After another hour of discussion, everyone at the meeting seemed to be in a slightly more positive frame of mind, although I could still see the signs of restrained shock on some of the faces. One of those faces was Frank's – a face that was usually a blazing tribute to a hale and hearty constitution. It was clear, however, that Frank had been shaken by the news. As the meeting broke up I made my way over to speak to him.

'I'm sure it will be all right,' I said, although I wasn't sure I knew what I meant by the words.

'Oh, I'm sure it will as well,' said Frank, mustering something resembling his usual hawkish grin. 'Fact is, I should have seen it coming more than most. What with having talked it through with that surveyor chap. Still, it wouldn't be a religion worth having if it didn't pick you up by the throat and turn you inside out every now and again, would it?'

As he said it, I could see that for him (as, I dare say, for a great many others as well) the stones of the church building were inseparable from the God that he worshipped. Whether this was good or bad, I really couldn't say – but it did appear to be true. We're all so frail, I thought. Even Lynda, with all her certainty about who did and who didn't have the Holy Spirit, like the rest of us, needed simple, tangible, familiar things to focus her mind on God. It was this same thought that reminded me of something I had meant to ask Frank.

'By the way,' I asked. 'What was the name of that carpenter chap you mentioned the other day? The one who carried out the repairs to the sanctuary rail. I think I may have another commission for him.'

'Carpenter? Oh, Peter, you mean. Peter Strang. Yes, of course. I have his phone number somewhere.'

Frank started feeling about his person for his note-book.

'Sorry, Michael,' he said, having frisked himself quite thoroughly. 'Don't seem to have it. I'll give you a ring when I get home. In the meantime, how about coming over to the pub for a quick drink. After all, we can't let this sort of thing get us down, can we?'

'That's the spirit,' said Canon George, joining us. 'I think I'll have one myself.'

* * *

I had just arrived home, and was talking to Cheryl about the meeting when the phone rang.

'That'll be Frank,' I said confidently.

But it wasn't. It was Chris Mulligan. He sounded very jolly but I wondered why he was phoning me at home. Last time it had been about a problem with his marriage.

'Well, after the mess I got you into with the Scotch,' he said, 'I thought I'd take no chances. Listen. I thought I'd say "thank you" properly this time. Me and Anne, see? We think we'll be getting back together again. I thought I could let you have something more useful than spirits this time. How about lunch? Both of you.'

As usual with Chris Mulligan, there was no expectation of any contrary view. I thanked him for the thought behind the offer, but was quite glad that we were otherwise engaged on the day he suggested.

'Sorry, Chris. That's the day of the Parish Summer Fayre. We'll be tied up all day at St Mark's. You could bake a cake for the Fayre if you like!'

Mulligan laughed and said he'd think about it. He was never the easiest of characters, but, as I put the phone down, I gave thanks for the fact that there seemed to be a promise of reconciliation in his private life.

As it turned out, Frank didn't ring until the next day, when he left a message on the answerphone with the address and telephone number of Peter Strang, the carpenter. I arranged to call on Peter at his workshop the following Saturday morning.

The workshop was only twenty minutes' walk from home, and even closer to St Mary's, but it took me to a part of the district I had not visited before. Following the road towards the centre of town, there was an alley on the right that appeared to go nowhere in particular. I had assumed it simply provided access to the backs of the tall buildings that fronted the road. It was this alley, however, that I had to follow.

After about fifty metres it turned sharply to the right again, and there, to my surprise, was a terrace of six small Victorian cottages, set back from the rest of the alley. The last one in the terrace was the home of Peter Strang, whom I had been directed to find by walking along the path at the side of the house to the workshop at the end of the garden.

The workshop was a building mainly of wood with the sort of old-fashioned and ramshackle appearance that seemed to concede nothing to modernity. The morning sunshine had drenched the garden in light, and the air was so quiet that I could hear the humming of insects as they threaded their way in and out of the tall flowers. Feeling that I was somehow caught in a time warp, and that this whole place had been conjured up from some idyllic past, I knocked at the door and was immediately called inside by a deep voice.

Peter Strang put down the chisel he was using and walked across the workshop, offering me a strong wide hand. His soft blue eyes nestled knowingly below a broad, tanned forehead, above which was a full head of grizzled grey hair. He looked to be about fifty, but could have been older.

'Reverend,' said Peter quietly, by way of greeting.

'Please,' I replied at once. 'Call me Michael.'

He waved me to a chair. I have never been a practical person, and as I sat down I gazed around in wonder at the serried ranks of tools and pieces of wood. I sucked in the smells of the place, savouring the air thick with peace. Orange sunlight, full of dust, sloped across one corner of the workshop, but otherwise the place was a pool of soft shadows. On a bench stood an almost complete small table, its legs beautifully turned, bracing themselves, ready to spring into life.

'You don't mind if we talk here,' said Peter, pulling a second chair from a dark corner.

'Not at all,' I said. 'I prefer it. Indeed, as I mentioned to you on the phone, I was hoping you might undertake a commission for me.'

50

Peter seemed to move his head slightly, which I took to be a sign that I should carry on.

'It's for the church really,' I added. 'I understand from Frank Foster that you've done a few things for the church. Most recently, the repair of the sanctuary rail at St Mary's.'

'Churches can be beautiful things,' said Peter, his gentle voice making no more sound than was necessary in the stillness of the workshop. 'Not always,' he continued. 'But where there is beauty, then we should do what we can to keep it.'

I nodded, ready to outline my commission, but Peter wanted to say more.

'I don't go to church,' he said.

People often said this to me. I had learned not to reply with an anxious-to-please 'Oh, that doesn't matter', and instead to wait for what else might be said. But Peter added nothing more, and so I pressed on with my request.

I explained that, currently, I was an ordained deacon in the church. How, at the beginning of October, I would be ordained a second time – as a priest. How I wanted to contribute something tangible to St Mary's, the church in which I spent most time. How the idea of giving something practical to the church seemed even more right now that the building itself would have to be closed for the next three or four months.

'What I have in mind, Peter, is a small stool on which I, or anyone else for that matter, can sit during services. At the moment, Canon George sits in what's known as the vicar's stall. When I'm ordained it will be the first time that there will be two priests in the church at the same time. I thought that I could perhaps sit on a stool especially made for the job.'

I paused for a moment, unsure as to whether I

should be conveying a practical briefing, or a fuller explanation of my feelings on the matter.

'The fact is,' I continued, 'I was hoping that you might be able to make something beautiful that would complement the other furniture in the sanctuary. If it could be made before the beginning of October, then I could use it for my first Eucharist – *wherever* that happens to take place. If St Mary's is still closed, it will probably be at St John's. In which case, I can bring the stool back up the hill when St Mary's finally reopens.'

Through all this Peter sat perfectly still, seeming to listen not only to what I was saying, but also to what I wasn't saying. He leaned across the top of the bench and took an old photograph album from a shelf on the wall. Flicking through it, he opened it at a page on which were three or four Polaroid photographs of stools.

'These are some of the stools I've made,' he said. 'That one's a bar stool. That one's a footstool. In terms of height, I suppose you want something in between.'

We started to define exactly what the stool should be like, which I took to be a sign that Peter was accepting the commission, even though we had not spoken about money. He started to make sketches on a large sheet of paper while I rambled on in a confused way about the sorts of things I liked and the sorts of things I didn't.

Fifteen minutes, and several sketches, later Peter had drawn a picture for a design of a stool that was made of oak and decorated with a solitary Celtic cross. I simply looked at him and smiled my approval. Somehow, Peter seemed to have cut through the surplus words of my talk and expressed a design which had previously been no more than an unformed idea inside my head. He responded to my smile with one of his own, and with that our meeting seemed to be over. I was conscious, however, that a price had still not been mentioned.

'What about the cost?' I said at last.

Peter's eyes seemed to be shining.

'Let's wait till I've made it, shall we?' he said. 'Then we can see if it's good. If it serves its purpose.'

I was about to object, for both our sakes, but there was an air of finality about the way Peter rose from his chair and picked up his chisel again. This was not the sort of basis on which I was used to conducting business, but for some reason it felt right.

'Can I come and see the work in progress?' I asked as I was leaving.

'I'm always here,' said Peter with the faintest of smiles. 'Except when I'm away.'

I took this to be a 'yes' and walked back through the sunlit garden to find my way home.

FOUR

Fayre Play

Now there are varieties of gifts.
1 Corinthians 12:4

WITH St Mary's closed for repairs, the parish celebration of Pentecost took place at St John's. It was a rather muted occasion and fell some way short of being the uplifting experience I had been looking for. The minds of most of the St Mary's people seemed to be on fundraising rather than on the coming of the Holy Spirit, and the immediate focus for their attention was the Saturday immediately following Pentecost – the day of the parish Summer Fayre.

The annual Summer Fayre was a joint event for the two churches, although it always took place at St Mary's because there was more room. The church at the top of the hill was blessed with a churchyard, an adjoining garden and large car park, whereas St John's sat cheek by jowl with several shops in the main thoroughfare.

In previous years, the Summer Fayre had occupied most of the available open space around St Mary's, although the building itself had been used for a number of arts and crafts stalls. This year, of course, was to be different. Scaffolding had been moved into the body of the church during the preceding week, and only Colin had access to the building for the day of the Fayre. We were therefore, more than ever before, dependent on having good weather.

God must have been smiling on us because I woke to a

bright sun in a clear blue sky. I had been lying in bed for only a few minutes, squinting at the world through the open curtains, when my daughter came into the room.

'C'mon, Daddy,' she said, noticing my barely open eyes and choosing to ignore the sleeping lump of her mother next to me. 'C'mon, Daddy. Let's go to the circus.'

'It's not a circus,' I said for the umpteenth time. 'It's a Summer Fayre.'

'Will there be a tightrope walker?' asked Amy.

'Not unless the vicar takes it into his head to do a few new tricks.'

'Not unless what?' said Amy.

'Nothing, darling. Daddy was just talking to himself,' I replied through tight lips.

'You know, Amy,' said a sleepy voice next to me. 'Just like when Daddy's preaching.'

'Thank you very much,' I said. 'And good morning to you too!'

Cheryl pulled the duvet further up over her head and proceeded to make snoring noises.

'Is there a zoo?' asked Amy with that imperturbable zeal that so often characterizes five-year-olds.

'Amy,' I said, trying to be understanding. 'I don't want to disappoint you, but I think that your expectations of this event may be a bit too high.'

'*What*'s too high?' said Amy, pulling a face.

'Daddy's expectations of your vocabulary, darling,' came the voice from below the covers.

'Come on, Amy,' I said, choosing to ignore the comment. 'Let's go and get some breakfast, shall we?'

'And some tea for Mummy?'

'Well, if you make it, I'll pour it over her head.'

Amy thought this was funny, so I decided to quit while I was ahead.

After having breakfast with my daughter, I showered, shaved and put on one of my more exuberant clerical shirts (the one with red and blue stripes), a cream linen suit, and a new Panama hat.

'You're not seriously going to wear that, are you?' said Cheryl supportively.

'Daddy's in a circus,' said Amy.

'You can say that again,' said my wife.

'I'll see you later, darling,' I said stoically. 'Amy, darling. Mummy will bring you along later. I've got to go and help get ready.'

Ten minutes later I arrived at St Mary's and was walking through the churchyard when I heard the voice of Colin hailing me.

'Father Michael, Father Michael! Coooeee!'

I looked around and could see no sign of him.

'Father Michael!' came the voice again. 'Up here! I'm in the tower.'

I looked up at the top of the church tower, shielding my eyes against the light. It was still only ten o'clock, but the sun was already strong. The Fayre was due to open at eleven and I could hear the busy sound of people setting up stalls and sideshows in the garden and car park.

'Is that you, Colin?' I called back, able only to make out a dark figure framed by one of the gothic arches near the top of the tower. 'What are you doing up there?'

'Bunting,' came the reply.

'Of course,' I muttered to myself, still unsure as to what he was up to. Bunting? Was that like abseiling? And had Colin bunted before?

'I've found the bunting we used around the church for the Queen's Jubilee,' called Colin.

'Oh, *that* bunting,' I said.

'I thought I could hang it from the tower to some-where else,' continued Colin. 'But I'm not sure there's anything much to tie it to. If I throw it down to you, perhaps we could just drape it elegantly around the outside of the church.'

I looked around to see if I could see anything to which the bunting could be fastened.

'Colin,' I called back. 'How long is the bunting?'

'I'm not sure,' he shouted. There must be a few hundred feet of it, I would have thought. With red and blue flags all the way along.'

'Hang on there a minute,' I called. 'I've an idea. I'll be back soon. Don't go away!'

Waving to Barbara Bailey and Doreen Butcher who were carrying boxes of crockery towards the car park, I made my way out of the churchyard, over the road, and into the block of flats opposite. My mission took longer than the minute I had promised Colin, but I was soon back at the foot of the tower.

'OK, Colin,' I shouted. 'Secure one end of it up there and then throw the rest down.'

Once the bunting had been safely thrown from on high, Colin left his perch and made his way down the spiral staircase, finally emerging into the sunlight wearing, as usual, his cassock.

'I have a cunning plan,' I said in answer to his quizzical look. 'Do you know Izzy Hutchings who lives on the second floor in Gracewell Court? Well, she's happy to have one end of the bunting fixed through her window. So all you've got to do is get this pile over the road and throw one end up to her.'

Seeing Colin's slightly horrified face, I added,

'Well, perhaps we could get someone to help you. Someone to help you carry it across the road. And someone to go up to Izzy's window to catch the end of it.'

'What about the traffic?' asked Colin in a tremulous voice.

'Don't worry about that,' I said breezily. 'You can lay the bunting across the road until you're ready to haul it into position.'

As I said this I saw a double-decker bus pass by, and the look of horror on Colin's face grew noticeably.

'And don't worry about the buses either,' I added quickly. 'I'm sure the bunting will be much higher than they are. Well, *fairly* sure, anyway!'

Colin appeared as if he were about to object, but by this point I felt committed to a plan that symbolically linked the church with one of its neighbouring buildings.

'Don't fret, Colin,' I said, clapping him on the shoulder, and hearing him splutter by way of reply.

'It will look very . . .' I continued as I made broad expansive gestures with my hands.

'very . . . well . . . celebratory, I suppose. Think of it as a sign of outreach. As a sign of the way we reach out to touch the lives of those who live around us.'

Colin clearly wished he had never shouted to me from the tower in the first place. But I was not to be put off. Spotting three familiar and young faces coming in at the gate, I decided to implicate them in the plan.

'Hey, you guys! Can you give us a hand?'

If Colin looked concerned about the enterprise before, he now looked mortified.

'Ah, splendid!' I said, looking down at Adam, Edwin and Gemma. 'Just the job! Now what I'd like you to do is help the verger fix this bunting between the church tower and the block of flats opposite. Do you think you can do that?'

'Is the Pope a Catholic?' said Adam, directing a wink in Colin's direction. Colin winced visibly.

'Is the Pope a Catholic?' I repeated, half to myself. 'The youth of today, eh, Colin!' I looked across to Colin, but he and his bunting were already under siege from Edwin.

'Do you want me to do a sign?' said Gemma loudly. 'I've got lots of paper and a big black pen for doing signs.'

'No, I don't think we want any signs, do we, Colin? Just a bit of help with the bunting.'

Gemma looked slightly disappointed, but quickly regained her spirits when she saw Edwin beginning to entangle the verger in the bunting.

'Well, I'll leave you chaps to it then,' I chirped merrily, heading off towards the back of the church and leaving Colin in the clutches of the intrepid scouts.

As I reached the other side of the church building the first thing I saw was the bouncy castle, which was being pumped full of air. This I guessed would be the focus of Amy's attention. With any luck, it would make up for the lack of any obvious circus acts.

I passed down the stone steps and into the main area of the garden and car park where I could see the results of the great activity that had clearly been going on for some time. My role was to be an encourager and *agent provocateur*, charged with getting as many people to part with as much of their money as possible. As such I would not be tied to any one stall or sideshow, but would have licence to roam around in a predatory manner, cajoling people into trying things which they might otherwise have been inclined to avoid. My first priority, however, was to check on everyone who was there and to review the general state of preparedness.

The first stall I came to was the tombola, where Alan Watts and Hilary Noble were stationed. Alan looked as if he had been there for hours, arranging and rearranging the items until he had them in a satisfactory order. It being a Saturday, Hilary was not dressed in her usual formal suit, but still managed to look anything but relaxed in tweeds and pearls.

At a sensible distance from the other attractions was the area in the corner of the car park where parishioners would be invited to throw wet sponges at volunteers. This year the honour of running the wet-sponge sideshow had fallen to the scouts, and I could see Jack and Don setting up.

'Good morning, gentlemen,' I called as I approached.

They looked up from arranging two chairs a few feet in front of a large tarpaulin which was draped over the wall.

'Michael,' said Jack. 'So it's you. I didn't recognize you at first. You look so . . . different.'

Don grunted, as if to suggest that 'different' wasn't the word *he* would have chosen.

'You haven't seen Adam, Edwin and Gemma, have you?' asked Jack. 'They said they would be here at ten.'

'Ah,' I replied knowingly. 'They're a bit tied up with Colin at the moment.' I looked back over my shoulder, but could see nothing of Gracewell Court from where I was standing. 'If that's all right with you,' I added. 'They're helping to put up a few decorations. They shouldn't be too long.'

'No problem,' said Jack. 'But I want to send them out for a couple more sponges when they arrive. Then between us, we're going to take turns at being on the receiving end. Bit of a lark, eh?'

I turned towards Don who looked as serious as always.

'A lark,' he echoed flatly. 'A bit of a lark.'

'Right then,' I said. 'Good luck. I'll be back later to throw a sponge at you myself.'

Moving away from the corner spot, I next came to a

table on which had been stuck a very large paper notice that said 'Wheel of Fortune'. There was, however, nothing on the table. Behind the table was John Burgess.

'Morning, John.'

John glowered back.

'The wheel,' he said slowly and mournfully. 'The wheel!'

'Yes?' I said, losing a little of my jollity at the sound of his ominous voice. 'What about the wheel?'

'The thing's fallen off,' said John with an air of finality. 'Off!'

I nodded sympathetically. I had seen the said wheel on a number of occasions. It was made of plywood and was about three feet wide. The face of the wheel was divided into eight numbered sections, and a large wooden arrow was fixed loosely in the middle. Players would pay fifty pence each to select one of the eight numbers, and when all eight were chosen the arrow would be spun. Winners received a bottle of cider or some other kind of fizzy drink. It was all very uncomplicated, but clearly depended on having the wheel in good working order.

'Would that be the arrow, John?' I asked as gently as I could. 'The thing that's fallen off?'

'Oh, woe,' intoned John, his eyes rolling in their sockets. 'It's a sign. A sign!'

I ventured the opinion that it was probably a sign of nothing more than the old age of the wheel in question, and that it could probably be repaired fairly easily. Indeed, as I was to find out, this was already happening. In carrying off the wheel, Rose had been intercepted by Frank who was at that very moment repairing the arrow, thereby giving the parish wheel of fortune several more years of life.

61

'Keep smiling,' I said to John. 'I'm sure it will be all right.' John shook his head meaningfully, and as I moved on I tried to remember whose idea it was that 'the prophets' should run the wheel of fortune.

'Or anything else, for that matter,' added Stephen Pickle, when I bumped into him a few seconds later. 'Come to think of it, I'm sure they volunteered. Yes, now I remember. John Burgess said he was going to rename it "Wheel of *Mis*fortune". Everyone whose number didn't come up would be condemned to looking at Alan's photos of his trip to the Holy Land.'

Stephen broke off being rude about Alan's photos to smile beatifically at the two Marys, who were heading in our direction carrying trays of cups and saucers.

'Oh, Michael! Stephen!' said Mary Brown, fluttering her eyelashes for all she was worth. 'You both look so splendid. So absolutely splendid!'

I looked at Stephen who was wearing a biretta with a flower stuck in it.

'Don't they look splendid, Mary?'

Mary West eyed us both suspiciously.

'We're on teas,' smiled Mary Brown.

'We're on valium,' said Stephen quietly. I nudged him heavily in the ribs.

'Well, that's splendid too,' I said supportively. 'Stephen and I will carry those for you, ladies. Won't we, Stephen?'

'Oh, yes, of course,' said Stephen, rubbing his bruised ribs.

'How are the preparations for the teas coming along?' I asked, as we walked four abreast towards the church hall.

'The teas will be fine,' said Mary West matter-of-factly. 'So will be the orange squashes and the fairy cakes.'

'And the home-made biscuits,' added Mary Brown.

'*And* the home-made biscuits,' echoed Mary West. 'But I *am* concerned that we have nothing more substantial to give people if they want some lunch while they're here. It would be nice if we could sell some sandwiches. I could even heat up some sausage rolls in the church hall kitchen. But when we had the meeting, Mary said she thought we should concentrate on teas and not on lunches.'

It was not said as a criticism, but the other Mary felt obliged to respond.

'Well, at least we know where we are with teas,' said Mary Brown, straightening her immaculate dress and pushing gingerly at her newly-curled hair. Stephen nodded seriously.

'You do know where you are with teas,' he repeated. I looked away, worried that I might giggle involuntarily.

'But as for lunches,' continued Mary Brown. 'There's only so much you can do with a quiche.'

I bit my bottom lip and nodded.

'People want more exciting things nowadays, don't they?' said Mary Brown, warming to her theme. 'Burgers and pizzas and those macho things.'

Stephen pushed out his chest and felt his biceps. I ignored him.

'What macho things?' I asked politely.

'You know. Those Mexican macho things,' said Mary.

'Oh, *those* macho things.' I tried to look understanding. 'Well, I'm sure your teas will go down a treat.'

'Just so long as the people aren't really hungry,' said Mary West resignedly.

'The people are always hungry,' said a deep voice

behind me. 'At least spiritually, they are. Our job is to feed them, and then to free them. I'm sure everything you do will contribute to that great aim, Mary.'

I turned round to see the vicar, Canon George, beaming at all of us.

'George,' I said. 'How are you?'

'Well, I'll feel a lot happier when I've got my pram sorted out. See you later.'

And with that he disappeared as quickly as he had appeared. The two Marys had begun to arrange the cups and saucers on the kitchen worktops, continually reassuring each other with comments like 'So much nicer than paper cups' and 'Well, everyone knows it tastes so much better out of a *proper* cup'.

'Pram?' I said. 'What pram?'

'When I asked him earlier what he was up to, he was very mysterious,' said Stephen. 'He told me "You will hear the sound of the vicar walking in the garden". He's obviously plotting something.'

We had made our way back out into the car park and, as Stephen went off to unload a crate of paperbacks from his car, I continued my perambulation of the sideshows. It was almost eleven o'clock, and the official opening of the Summer Fayre was only minutes away. I turned to my right and found Geoffrey and Amanda Newton setting up a coconut shy.

'Ah, Michael,' crooned Geoffrey. 'You're just in time to have first go at the theological shy.'

'*Theological* shy?' I said, fearing the worst.

'You see those six coconuts on stands,' said Amanda. 'Well, Geoffrey and I thought we could put labels on them like "Virgin Birth" . . .'

'Or "Bodily Resurrection",' added Geoffrey briskly. 'And then people could have a go at knocking down traditional Christian doctrines.'

I looked around nervously to make sure that no one else had overheard these comments.

'Geoffrey, Amanda,' I said softly and patiently. 'You *are* joking, aren't you?'

They both leaned forward earnestly.

'Yes, we're joking,' they said softly and patiently.

I forced a smile, made my excuses and moved on. One day, I thought, Geoffrey and Amanda are going to go too far.

Fortunately Lynda's bookstall had not been positioned next to the coconut shy. The next person I met was Joy Bartholomew who was standing behind a trestle-table on which were numerous home-made cakes, all neatly wrapped in see-through film and price-marked.

'That's quite a display of cakes!' I said, stating the obvious.

'And yet Jane's father never did like marzipan,' said Joy.

'Very good,' I said supportively, and moved quickly on.

Next to Joy was Lynda's bookstall, and Lynda and a friend were putting the last few books in place. It was a mixture of second-hand books which had been donated by parishioners and new Christian books, all of which were evangelical in character. Lynda noticed the look on my face as I perused the various Christian titles that she had spread out.

'Anything there you fancy, Michael?'

'Do you have anything a bit less . . . I mean, a bit more . . .?'

'A bit less or more what? We've some slightly less *educational* books in a brown cardboard box over here. But we'll only start putting *those* out if we get desperate.'

'Right,' I said. 'Well, whatever you think best.'

I was about to suggest to Lynda that we should be trying to sell as many books as possible, almost regardless of their flavour, but my train of thought was broken by the sound of smashing crockery. About fifteen feet the other side of the bookstall was the crockery-smashing area where, for a small sum, you could buy three wooden blocks to hurl at several shelves of crockery. 'Very therapeutic,' I remember Canon George saying when the idea first came up. I was interested, however, to see who was 'manning' the enterprise.

If you had asked me to name the two people I would have least expected to be running the crockery stall, it would have been Doreen Butcher and Barbara Bailey. In their different ways, their very proper appearances and their staunchly traditional outlooks would have led me to the conclusion that the smashing of crockery was both too extrovert and too iconoclastic.

On the contrary, however, they seemed to be setting about their task with a purpose that I could not have imagined of a crockery-smashing fanatic. By now the Fayre was under way, and the first visitors were moving between the various activities.

'Roll up, roll up,' bellowed Doreen through cupped hands. 'Come and have a smashing time!'

'Oh, that's very good, Doreen,' said Barbara regally. 'Smashing time. Very good indeed!'

I waved at them both, and they (still looking slightly incongruous in floral dresses) waved back.

'Michael,' called Barbara. 'Come and get smashed!'

'No, dear,' corrected Doreen. 'It's "Come and have a smashing time." Not "Come and get smashed".'

'Righto!' said Barbara, before calling out to me once again.

'A bit later,' I called back, conscious that I wanted to

find out whether the bunting had been successfully unfurled. I walked back towards the corner where I had left the scout masters and their wet sponges.

'Wotcha!' called a fair-haired boy with glasses as I approached.

'Hiya!' said a taller boy with red hair.

Adam and Edwin had only just arrived back after helping Colin with the bunting.

'Where's Gemma?' I asked, looking around.

'She's still over at Mrs Wotsit's,' said Adam.

'She said she wanted to add a finishing touch.'

'What sort of finishing touch?' I said, feeling slightly uncomfortable that Gemma had not returned with the others.

'Yes,' said Jack, getting up from a chair in front of a large tarpaulin, and dripping water from every inch of his weather-beaten skin. 'What exactly have you lot been up to?'

There was no time for an answer, however, because at that very moment the air was pierced by a loud crackling noise, followed by the voice of Canon George booming around the church grounds.

'GOOD MORNING AND WELCOME TO ST MARY'S!'

Jack and I looked at one another.

'Where's that coming from?' I said. 'It sounded as if it was coming from the heavens!'

Jack looked up and pointed a wet finger towards the other end of the car park. I turned to see Canon George emerging through the gate from the garden pushing an old pram in front of him. In the pram was an amplifier and a large speaker, and fixed to the handle of the pram with a quantity of sticky tape was one of the microphones from the church.

'WELCOME TO OUR PARISH FETE, AND CAN I BEGIN BY SAYING THAT . . .'

From then on things seemed to happen very quickly. No sooner had Canon George reached a central position in the midst of the sideshows and stalls – thus attracting the attention of the not inconsiderable number of people who had now arrived – when Frank Foster suddenly appeared at his shoulder.

The conversation that ensued between them might have remained something of a mystery for ever had it not been for the fact that Canon George found himself unable to turn off the microphone. Thus it was that the following words were broadcast very loudly across the entire Summer Fayre.

'EXCUSE ME, GEORGE.'

'YES, FRANK.'

'I'M NOT SURE WHOSE IDEA IT WAS, BUT I THINK WE OUGHT TO REMOVE THE BUNTING WHICH IS STRETCHED FROM THE CHURCH TOWER TO THE BLOCK OF FLATS OPPOSITE.'

'BUNTING? CHURCH TOWER?'

Canon George, perplexed, looked around for some hint of what was happening. Frank carried on.

'IT SEEMS TO BE CAUSING SOME . . . UNEASE.'

'BUNTING? UNEASE?'

I felt the moment had passed when I might usefully have been able to intervene, and so I remained where I was, biting my bottom lip. Frank was still explaining.

'WELL, IT'S NOT SO MUCH THE BUNTING ITSELF, AS RATHER THE SIGN THAT'S HANGING FROM IT.'

'SIGN?'

'YES. IT SAYS, "COME TO THE ST MARY'S SUMMER FAYRE – IT'S WELL BAD".'

'WELL BAD?'

Next to me Adam and Edwin were creased up with laughter.

'Nice one, Gemma!' said Edwin.

'Don't the vicar know that "bad" means "good"?' asked Adam.

'What?' I said, not sure that I was hearing everything right. 'I think I'd better . . .'

I started to push my way through the growing crowd to where Canon George was standing looking bemused, but suddenly I felt a restraining hand on my arm. I looked round.

'I'm sorry, Mary,' I said, finding that Mary Brown had fastened herself to me, 'but I've got a small crisis to sort out.'

'*You*'ve got a crisis to sort out,' said Mary, her heavily made-up eyes almost bulging out of her head. '*We*'ve got a crisis. I'm afraid Mary was right! Everyone's eating the food!'

I looked at her in exasperation.

'Isn't that what it's there for?'

'But we're going to run out!'

'Mary!' I almost choked, looking round and seeing that the vicar was disappearing back through the gate at the end of the car park. 'Please! I'll sort something out. Honest!'

I freed myself from her clutches and started to thread my way through the mêlée. I had just reached the gate, when I found my way barred by a thick-set man who was just coming in.

'Michael!'

Hearing my name, I looked up into a face I knew well.

'Chris! Chris Mulligan! What on earth are *you* doing here?'

'Now, what sort of friendly greeting is *that*?'

'But Chris, you don't come to church things! You certainly don't come to church things *here*. What's going on?'

Chris Mulligan grinned at me, showing off a set of uneven teeth. He put his arm around my shoulder, looked me up and down, pulled a face at the way I was dressed, and led me away from the gate.

'Thought I'd surprise you, Reverend,' he said. 'As I said on the phone last time we spoke, I think I owe you one after that business with the Scotch. And seeing as today you couldn't get away to lunch – well, I thought I'd bring lunch to *you*. And to all your mates as well!'

Mulligan laughed his usual bluff laugh.

'Come on,' he said. 'Come and help me unload.'

'Unload? Unload what?'

'The pizzas, of course. You didn't think I came all this way just to say hello, did you? I figured if you didn't want the Scotch, you might want some pizzas. You know, so you could cook them up and sell them as part of the fête or whatever this thing is.'

He gazed around him, his face full of bemusement at what he saw. Once I realized what he was saying, I wanted to thank him, but the words froze on my lips. 'Chris . . .' was all I could get out. Mulligan saw my confusion.

'Not a word,' he said. 'Don't say a word. Look, it's no skin off *my* nose. I've got pizzas coming out of my ears. The least I can do is try to feed some of your flock. Come on. They're in the boot of the car. All wrapped up in dry ice. Now, where do you want them?'

As I moved forward to follow Chris Mulligan, I turned round to try to find Mary Brown again. She was an easy figure to pick out.

'Mary,' I called. 'Put the oven on in the hall kitchen. I think we should be able to feed everyone after all.'

70

FIVE

The Wood for the Trees

'Thus you will know them by their fruits.'
Matthew 7:20

THE end of May had seen Canon George and Stephen Pickle embarking on a series of joint Sunday morning services at St John's. By the middle of June, however, it was clear that the vicar's call for unity in the worship of the parish had met with a less than enthusiastic response. No more than half the St Mary's regulars were attending the combined services, and several of those appeared to be doing so only with somewhat bad grace.

Thus it was that, after a three-week trial, Canon George bowed to the inevitable and announced that he would be exploring ways in which St Mary's Sunday morning services could be held in St Mary's church hall. This announcement aroused the immediate interest of most of the members of the St Mary's congregation, and there was no shortage of volunteers when Canon George asked for help in planning the first service. A meeting was arranged at the vicarage for an evening during the following week, and Canon George asked if I would act as secretary and make a record of what was agreed.

As was the case with most of my evening meetings, I arrived at the vicarage straight from work without having had a chance to see Cheryl or Amy. Frank opened the door and his first comment related to what I was wearing – a dark grey polo shirt and pale grey shorts.

'Evening, Michael,' he said. 'You're looking relaxed. On holiday?'

'No,' I replied, 'I've come straight from work.'

Frank looked me up and down once more, and so I felt bound to add, 'I wasn't seeing any clients today. Suits and ties are mainly for *their* benefit. Most of them would feel they couldn't trust a man in shorts.'

Frank smiled and looked as if he could understand why. I walked past him to the lounge where the other volunteers were ready and waiting. As I sat down and looked around I noticed all the people that I would have expected to be part of a worship planning group at St Mary's: Colin the verger, Barbara the sacristan, Malcolm the organist, Doreen representing the 'sidesmen', Penny representing the Sunday School and 'the young people', Lynda, Frank, and, of course, Canon George.

The vicar welcomed us and then led us in prayer, before throwing open the discussion in order to, as he put it, 'gauge the temperature' on the subject of worship in the hall. Lynda, who was never backward in coming forward, was the first to speak.

'I think it's a wonderful thing. A wonderful opportunity. God has given us this chance, and we must take it and use it. I'm looking forward to a new, open and informal style of worship in the church hall. A style of worship that will really allow the Holy Spirit to work through all of us. A style of worship that will inspire us. A style of worship that we will want to keep when we move back into the church building.'

Lynda stopped there, but I had the impression that she could have gone on all night. I looked around. There was some noticeable nodding from Penny who was mumbling some of Lynda's words to herself: 'Opportunity, yes. Informal, yes. Inspire, yes. Splendid.'

Otherwise there did not seem to be a great deal of enthusiasm for what had been said.

Doreen and Barbara were looking down their respective noses and glancing at each other in that 'Well! Honestly!' sort of way. Colin was rocking himself backwards and forwards with his eyebrows raised as if to say, 'Well, while that might seem a good idea to *some* people . . .' Malcolm was cleaning his spectacles on a dubious-looking handkerchief and staring around at everyone with a look of happy vacancy.

'What do you mean by "informal"?' said Frank, whose face betrayed only his usual good humour and practical nature.

Doreen stiffened her back and barked, 'If anyone so much as mentions liturgical dance . . .'

Everyone turned towards Doreen, but her words ebbed away into a disgusted exhalation of breath. She looked somewhat embarrassed that one of her dearest prejudices had managed to betray itself quite so demonstratively.

'Yes, Lynda,' said Canon George, in his soft and calming way. 'Picking up Frank's point, how "informal" is "informal" in your mind?'

Lynda was clearly less than comfortable with the kind of response that her opening comments had engendered in some of the others present.

'Well, I was rather assuming – as we were not going to be in the church building – that the Sunday service could be completely different. In fact, I was rather hoping that it might be everything that a Sunday service normally *isn't*. You know, no formal structure or liturgy as such, but rather an openness to the Holy Spirit. Lots of singing – choruses preferably – and readings and prayers and so on. But no Lord's Supper as such.'

'No Communion?' squawked Barbara.

'No Eucharist?' piped Malcolm.

'No Mass?' choked Colin.

I just stopped myself from saying 'No problem', and instead made sure that my notes were recording the general tenor of a discussion which had thrown us right into the heart of controversy within its first few minutes.

'May I speak?' asked Doreen. It was something of a rhetorical question. 'My own expectations of a service in the hall – *and*, I presume, the expectations of others present here tonight . . .' She paused to look round at the other faces, one or two of which were inclined in her direction as if to say, 'That's it, Doreen. You tell them!'

'. . . *my* expectations are that the service will be as close as possible to what we *normally* do – and have done for some time – at St Mary's. It will therefore be a way of preserving the tradition in which we have all been succoured, and not an opportunity for over-turning it.'

Lynda bridled at this comment.

'I'm not trying to overturn *any* tradition,' she said. 'I simply hoped that we might *add* to it. Traditions are, after all, only what you make them.'

'But Doreen is right,' said Barbara with her usual imperturbable confidence. 'The reason we were not entirely happy with the services at St John's was not that we were opposed to parish unity. It was all to do with tradition. It's not what Doreen or I *think* that is important. What's important is our tradition – the one we've grown up with. We have – *all* of us have – a duty to preserve the tradition of St Mary's.'

'A duty to whom?' asked Penny. 'Surely not to God. And perhaps not to the majority of people in this

74

parish either. For all we know, they might prefer the type of service that Lynda's suggesting. We'll never know unless we try. And, after all, it's only for a few months.'

It was clear that tempers were already beginning to get a little frayed – and it was at this point that Canon George turned to me and said, 'Do you think you've managed to capture the essence of the debate so far, Michael?'

Instead of replying as I felt – that most of the people present couldn't see beyond the end of their noses – I prevaricated and said, 'I think there are a number of issues here, and we clearly need to reflect as broad a position as possible.'

OK, I know. It was a bit like saying 'I abdicate all responsibility. Please! I just want a quiet life.' Sometimes, however, that's exactly how I felt in church meetings of this kind after a long day at the office. Fortunately, Canon George had a more patient and constructive way of dealing with things.

'Can I suggest that we concentrate less on what might divide us, and more on what might unite us?' he said. 'Malcolm, what about the music? How will that be affected by using the hall, and how can we turn the situation to good effect by making the most of what the Lord has given us in musical gifts?'

The question seemed to take Malcolm completely unawares. He crossed his arms meaningfully.

'Well, there won't be any organ, of course.'

There was a short pause, during which the combined thoughts of everyone else present winged their way towards Malcolm's head with the message, 'Thank you, Malcolm. I think we'd worked *that* one out for ourselves.'

'The piano in the hall's a bit ropey,' Malcolm

continued at last. 'But I think we can compensate by doing two things. First, by making sure we sing well-known hymns so that the burden, as it were, on the piano and the choir is reduced. And, secondly, by introducing some other instruments. I know there are a few people in the congregation who can play instruments. I could ask them to join in. We could have something of a little band!'

I could see that the more Malcolm thought about it, the more enthusiastic he became about the new musical horizons opened up by the lack of the organ.

'Heaven preserve us from guitars!' sighed Barbara very loudly.

'And tambourines!' added Doreen.

'I've never been keen on xylophones,' mused Colin.

'No, I don't think you understand, Colin,' said Barbara, who felt that Colin's lack of prescience was a genetic weakness of vergers. 'We're not criticizing the instruments as instruments. We're criticizing them for what they *represent*. In churches, that is. Guitars and tambourines are not part of our tradition.'

'Oh,' said Colin meekly. 'I see.'

Canon George could see that Lynda was about to leap back into the fray, but he stayed her with the slightest movement of his hand.

'Let's ask Malcolm what he has in mind before we reach any conclusions, shall we?' said the vicar. 'Malcolm?'

Malcolm looked to all intents and purposes as if he had nothing in mind other than the prospect of spending the following Saturday with his camera and liver-sausage sandwiches at Clapham Junction, train-spotting.

'Welllllll,' said the organist ruminatively. 'We could have at least a little ensemble of piano, flute and percussion.'

'Percussion! There! I knew it!' said Barbara.

'What sort of percussion?' asked Frank, who had been a drummer in an army band.

'Well, Geoffrey Newton is rather good on maracas, I believe,' ventured Malcolm.

'Maracas!'

It was something of a muted shriek from Barbara and Doreen. Colin scratched his chin thoughtfully, not wanting to be seen as intolerant.

'Maracas for the Mass,' he said thoughtfully. 'Hmmmmm. Yessss. Well, I can see that that *would* be something of a departure from tradition.'

Church meetings have a tendency to go on and on. Church meetings about *worship* tend to go on and on and *on*. The meeting at the vicarage that evening did not finish until eleven o'clock. Had it not been for the smoothing-over that Canon George was almost permanently required to perform, I dare say that things could have gone on into the early hours of the morning.

By eleven, however, a sort of plan had been agreed. It owed more to the traditional than it did to the new, but was nevertheless something of a compromise. After a closing prayer, we left for our homes, all of us (in our own different ways) looking forward to the following Sunday and our first service in St Mary's church hall.

* * *

Sunday morning began ominously. The telephone rang at a quarter to eight. It was Kay, the vicar's wife. Canon George had been up all night with 'd and v' – diarrhoea and vomiting. He was still feeling very ill and the doctor had been called out. Very sorry, and all that, but I would have to take the service.

77

I heard myself saying 'I do hope he's all right' and 'Send him my love', but my mind was racing. Would I be able to lead the service in the church hall, knowing how much argument there had been about its planning, and how important Canon George's calm authority was always likely to be in these kinds of circumstances?

It was not simply that I was inexperienced in leading worship on my own. It was not even that I was unsure as to how I should handle an innovative occasion in the church hall. It was more that the service had been planned as a Eucharist. As I was a deacon, and still more than two months away from being ordained a second time as a priest, I was acutely aware that I would not be able to consecrate the bread and the wine.

That meant that there were two options open to me. First, I could use reserved sacrament. That is, I could use bread – or more likely, wafers – and wine that had already been consecrated. The aumbry (a small locked compartment set into the wall of the side chapel) contained a limited number of consecrated wafers and a small flask of wine. These were renewed by Canon George each week, and were, in the intervening time, used in those situations when anyone other than a priest took communion to someone at home.

The trouble with this option was that there would be no more than about twenty wafers in the aumbry and a corresponding amount of consecrated wine. This would be far too small an amount to feed the Sunday morning congregation of St Mary's, even if fewer than usual turned up to this first service in the church hall. Had Canon George not been so obviously unwell, I might have asked him to consecrate some more bread and wine before the service began. But, given his predicament, such a request was clearly not realistic.

My second option was to make the service something other than a Eucharist. The mere thought of this made me unhappy because I knew how central the Eucharist was to the lives of those who worshipped at St Mary's. That applied to the 'freer' members of the congregation – people like Lynda, Penny and Geoffrey – as much as it did to the more traditional. It would be doubly difficult, given the amount of time that we had spent together at the worship meeting working out how the Eucharist could best be arranged within the confines of the church hall.

In the end I knew that I had no real choice at all. I brightened, however, when I realized that the timing of the service provided an opportunity to cater for those for whom the *form* of the worship, rather than its location, was the key point at issue. The Sunday morning service at St Mary's always began half an hour before the one at St John's. I had no doubt that people would arrive earlier than normal on this particular occasion, following all the hullabaloo about it being the first service back on St Mary's territory. I would therefore have the opportunity of explaining the situation to everyone at half past nine. Those who wanted their Sunday morning Eucharist as usual would have time to drive or walk the extra half-mile down the hill to St John's. Any who chose not to do this would have the option of taking part in a more extemporary service up the hill at St Mary's. Malcolm, I was sure, would be able to rustle up a few more hymns at short notice, and I could dig out a few more prayers. In effect, the resumption of normal service at St Mary's would be postponed for just one more week, by which time I felt sure Canon George's dicky tummy would have recovered.

I went through the rationale in my head once again and then telephoned Malcolm. The phone seemed to ring for ages before a very sleepy voice simply said 'Potts'. I explained the situation to him – that the service would not, after all, be a Eucharist – and I asked him to think of ways in which we could introduce some more music and hymns into the worship. I, for my part, I explained, would prepare some more prayers that we could say together.

When I arrived at St Mary's I went straight to the church hall. I decided that to call at the vicarage, even simply to wish Canon George well, might not be the best use of my time. I could do that after the service – and after the vicar had been seen by the doctor on duty.

In the church hall I found Frank, Geoffrey and Trevor Copeland putting the finishing touches to the arrangement of chairs. A table had been placed in a central position and covered with a cloth. Around it the chairs had been placed in a wide semicircle five rows deep. An aisle which was about three feet across dissected the semicircle and led from the door to the table, behind which were two chairs. To one side of the semicircle stood the piano and the places for the other musicians, and alongside those were ten more chairs pushed against the far wall where the choir was to sit.

Frank came towards me, his ruddy face looking more purple than usual after the exertions of the furniture-moving.

'Bad news about the vicar,' he said in a voice that seemed almost never to lose its good humour. 'I saw Kay just as I arrived. Still, lucky we've got you, that's what I say.' He slapped me affectionately on the shoulder. 'You'd better let me know what you want doing, Michael.'

Geoffrey and Trevor had finished moving chairs and were looking across to me as if expecting some further instructions.

'That looks great,' I said, trying to exude more confidence than I felt. 'I think that's probably all for now, thanks very much. I need to talk to Malcolm about the shape and content of the service. That's the priority now, I think. You know it's not going to be a Eucharist, don't you?'

I said these last words rather warily, but Frank, Geoffrey and Trevor simply nodded and said 'Right' and 'OK'. I was about to ask them whether they thought most people would leave for St John's on hearing the news, but at that moment Malcolm arrived, looking for all the world as if he had just got out of bed. My observation probably did him an injustice, because he threw his anorak into the corner with gay abandon, and immediately proceeded to show me a selection of extra hymns and music that he had put together following my call.

I glanced at my watch. It was ten minutes to nine. Worship was due to begin at half past nine. I asked Frank to help Malcolm and me choose the music and prayers, and the three of us sat down around the piano. As Frank was churchwarden I felt I could trust him to represent the views of many of the regular church-goers at St Mary's.

We decided that we would follow the format of the Eucharist service up to and including the Sharing of the Peace. Certain people would already have been approached to do the Scripture readings for the day and the Prayers of Intercession, and we didn't want to make changes unnecessarily. Following the Sharing of the Peace there would be a hymn as usual, after which I would use some prayers of self-offering that would, I hoped, help focus the worship on the self-giving involved in Christian life. I would then initiate a short silence for private prayer, which would end with a meditative piece of music played on the piano and flute by Malcolm and Julie, one of the members of the youth group. This would lead into two Taizé chants and two choruses which, Malcolm assured me, would be picked up easily by the congregation. I would then draw the whole thing together with two more short prayers, before leading the congregation in the Lord's Prayer.

As we talked I was surprised by how well the various pieces seemed to be fitting together and, as Malcolm rushed off to make photocopies of the chants and choruses in the parish office, I began to feel for the first time that morning that the Holy Spirit really *was* working with us.

I had to remember, however, that this service would still contain several elements of the more traditional approach at St Mary's – as had been agreed at the evening meeting several days before. For example, the choir members would be wearing their cassocks and surplices. They were also to be led in procession as usual, even though it would require them to gather outside the hall, from where they would move along the makeshift aisle and round to the chairs pushed against the wall.

At a quarter past nine I took myself off to the toilet for five minutes of peace and quiet. From there I went to the kitchen where I had hung my vestments on the fridge. At twenty-five past nine I walked nervously out into the body of the hall to make my announcement about the vicar.

My feeling of nervousness was heightened when I saw how many people had assembled. Not only was every seat taken, but people were actually standing all the way along the back of the hall and sitting in the aisle. I had never seen the place so packed.

As I took my place in front of the table, the hum of chattering voices gradually died down until a kind of hush hung in the air. Somehow I was aware that the story of Canon George's sickness had already worked its way around the hall, and so I was not surprised when my announcement of his indisposition was met mainly by knowing looks and confirmatory nods.

I carried on to say that the service this morning would not be a Eucharist, and made it clear that it would be perfectly understandable if people felt that they would rather make the move to St John's, where the service was due to begin in half an hour. I and the others would carry on, I said, with our plans for a slightly different service here in St Mary's hall for those who did not want to make the journey down the hill.

I stopped and waited. No one moved.

'So,' I continued, 'please feel free to go now to our other church for the parish Sunday morning Eucharist. I'm sure there will be places in cars available for those who don't fancy the walk.'

I stopped again. Still no one moved. I looked around nervously, trying to make eye contact with those whom I felt were likely to be the firmest advocates of the Sunday Eucharist – Colin, Barbara, Doreen. They were there all right. What's more, they were all fixed firmly to their seats, betraying not the merest hint of doing anything other than staying for the service in St Mary's hall.

In the end, my waiting and the accompanying silence became embarrassing. There was nothing for it, I decided. I would have to accept that no one was leaving. No one was deserting the sinking ship. We would have to begin, after all, as we had planned. I gave the signal to Malcolm, who started to play the introduction to 'Come, let us join our cheerful songs with angels round the throne'.

As the first notes echoed around, the door was flung open, and Maurice the crucifer, complete with his eye-patch and cross, marched forward into the hall, followed by the massed ranks of the choir who had been loitering outside ready for the triumphal entry.

Unfortunately, from their point of view, the way was barred by those members of the congregation who, in their unexpectedly high numbers, had filled the aisle. As Maurice came to an almost immediate halt the situation was only too clear to all concerned. The assembled squadron of choristers, bowing to the inevitable, dispersed to right and left in various attempts to thread their way to the chairs which had been set aside for their use.

From then on, things went fairly smoothly. We had the opening prayers. Dawn Copeland, Trevor's wife and mother of four young children, read the Epistle. We then sang 'Lord of the dance' to the accompaniment of piano, flute, and – yes! – maracas. (Never before or since have I seen a human being shake quite so much as Geoffrey did as he maraca'ed his way through the choruses.) After that Bill, one of the parish readers, read the gospel – 'a good tree cannot bear bad fruit, nor can a bad tree bear good fruit'. Then it was time for the sermon. I looked at Bill and Bill looked back at me, and in one horrible moment I suddenly realized what I had somehow managed to overlook right up to that point. The sermon was to have been preached by Canon George. In his absence, the honour clearly fell to me, his deputy.

I rose slowly to my feet, and looked around at the

expectant faces. Oh Lord, I thought. If ever there was a time for the Holy Spirit to be sent down upon my head, now was it. Help!

Needless to say, my sermon was off the cuff and spoken without much prior thought. I began falteringly, waffling on about how things had gone against us – against us all in the church community. How things had conspired to stop us from worshipping: the closure of the church building, and now the unavailability of the vicar. Here we were, without our natural leader, without our natural place of worship. And yet, in a way, that was just it. *Here we were!* In spite of those things, in spite of the fact that many of us could probably think of all sorts of reasons for not being here – *here we were.* Those who were keen on the ritual of liturgy and on dressing up were here alongside those for whom the chief delight of the morning would be Geoffrey's maracas!

The more I said, the more I relaxed. And the more I relaxed, the more I felt the Holy Spirit working through me, helping me along, almost whispering in my ear the words I should speak. I started to talk of what I could remember of the gospel reading. How we, the community of faith in this place, were a good tree. That how, no matter what our differences might be, if we stayed true to that faith we would always be able to produce good fruit in this place. Regardless of the building, regardless almost of the clergy, the fact remained that the Holy Spirit was alive in every one of us, and that we should never put too narrow an interpretation on the way that Spirit would express itself in the world.

As the words tumbled from my mouth, and as I saw the appreciative looks on people's faces as the message appeared to strike a chord with them, I began to feel quite intoxicated by what I was saying. And then, at the very moment when I felt as if I could have gone on all morning, the words stopped.

I had been on my feet for no more than five minutes, probably less. I stood, swaying slightly, bereft of the sudden eloquence that had transformed me from nervous deacon to impassioned preacher. The faces were still turned towards me, waiting for more, and for a few seconds I wavered, desperately trying to think of a way in which I could finish.

But it was over. And perhaps an enforced and self-conscious silence was the only fitting ending. I turned around awkwardly to pick up my papers from the chair, and when I spoke again it was to read with a strained and slow voice the notices for the week.

'Thank you,' I began, not sure what else I could say. 'There's just one notice that isn't on your sheets, and that concerns Harvest Festival. Now you're probably all thinking that Harvest Festival is a long way off, but it's not really. And, in a way, it ties in well with today's theme of fruits. This year we are going to reintroduce the idea of a Harvest Supper here in the church hall, just like some of you may remember from a few years' back.'

There were a few nods and smiles.

'This year, however,' I added, 'there will be a difference. We felt that the fruits of the parish were likely to be expressed in all sorts of different ways so we thought we would have a parish talent show to provide some cabaret at the Harvest Supper. We haven't yet worked out the details – but watch this space. It could be a night to remember!'

I managed a chuckle. The faces around me looked rather more dubious than enthusiastic at the idea.

'Anyway,' I said, 'that's something to look forward

to. For now, let's all rejoice in the fact that we are here together. Let's continue our worship by standing to proclaim our faith.'

In place of my single voice, thinned and frayed by nerves and the sermon, the hall was filled with the sound of more than a hundred voices ringing out together, 'We believe in one God . . .'

SIX

Giving Up the Ghost

When the disciples saw him walking on the sea,
they were terrified, saying, 'It is a ghost!' And
they cried out in fear. Matthew 14:26

ONE evening at the end of July I had gone straight to church from the office to do some parish work in the vestry. The repairs to the church structure did not affect the vestry, and I was able to let myself in and out without having to enter the main body of the building. I had finished working on the baptism forms and register, and was walking back through the car park of St Mary's, when I saw some lights on in the church hall. It was shortly before nine o'clock when I went over to investigate.

Inside I found a small group of scouts and scout leaders laying out various bags, ground sheets, and other pieces of camping paraphernalia.

'Evening, squire,' called Jack from where he was squatting on the floor folding the fly sheet of a tent. Don looked up from his clipboard and grunted a greeting in my direction.

'Hello, everyone,' I called, peering round at the several small faces that looked up at me. Among the group I noticed the three scouts who had helped with the bunting at the Summer Fayre – Adam, Edwin and Gemma.

Jack slid the folded fly sheet into a canvas bag and then levered himself off the floor.

'When are you off to camp?' I asked. 'Is it tomorrow?'

'Day after,' said Jack. 'But we want to get all this stuff ready and stowed away a full day before we leave. And you're just the chap we wanted to see before we went.'

'Me?' I laughed. 'You must be joking. As you may have noticed, I'm not renowned for my camping expertise.'

'Oh, it's nothing to do with camping,' said Jack. 'It's to do with the church. Which is why we thought it was right up your street. Have you got a few minutes?'

I looked at my watch. Amy was probably already asleep. Another day without the time to talk to my daughter. Cheryl and I were getting used to the idea of seeing less of each other in the evenings, and late suppers together were becoming something of a happy routine. But I couldn't pretend that our new life was without its cost.

'Sure,' I said. 'Why not?'

Jack winked at me as a sign of appreciation, and then turned his head to shout something over his shoulder. It wasn't exactly a surprise when I heard him call just three names. By now I had begun to realize that my fate was somehow linked with the lives of Adam, Edwin and Gemma.

All three looked pleased to be relieved of their packing duty as they greeted me with wide and cheeky smiles. Adam looked even more freckled than I remembered, presumably a tribute to the good weather that we had had all through July. Edwin squinted at me over the top of his glasses. Gemma fixed me with a serious stare.

'Hi, guys,' I said, trying to sound as cool as I could.

'Hiya!' came the concerted reply.

Jack shepherded the three scouts on to some nearby chairs, and I propped myself up against one of the tables.

'These three have had an idea, and they wanted to talk to you about it,' said Jack. 'OK, Adam, why don't you tell Michael what it's all about?'

In the far corner of the hall I could see Don and a small, plump boy wrestling with a tent pole. I looked back down at Adam's face and mop of ginger hair as he began to tell me about the idea.

'It's about the ghost,' he began.

'The Holy Ghost?' I prompted.

'Nah!' whined Edwin. 'Not the Only Ghost. Not him. We mean the one in the church.'

'Look, I'*m* telling him, aren't I?' complained Adam.

I nodded and fixed my gaze on Adam.

'The one in the church,' repeated Adam. 'When you showed us round, we heard about the ghost. The old man who was blown up by a bomb in the war.'

'He might not have been blown up,' added Gemma. 'There was no proof that he was blown up.'

'Well, he wasn't ever seen again,' continued Adam. 'And that probably means he was blown up.'

I tried to remember as much as I could about Jack's story of the vagrant who had lived rough around St Mary's in 1940.

'You see,' Adam went on purposefully, 'We were thinking about the ghost and how we'd like to see it, and then Gemma thought of a way we *could*. See it, I mean.'

By now I was fixated by what the terrible trio had cooked up – rather as a mouse must feel when a cat has it by the tail.

'Go on,' I said.

Gemma looked unusually abashed and noticeably less confident than I had remembered her to be.

'Well,' she said. 'It was when we heard that the church was falling down and that everyone had to try to think of ideas for getting money to pay to have it fixed. I thought we could be sponsored. You know. People could pay us 50p an hour or something.'

I glanced at Jack, but he was looking at Gemma. In the end I was forced to ask for clarification.

'50p an hour for doing *what* exactly?' I asked.

'For the ghost watch, of course,' said Edwin impatiently.

'Ghost *what*?' I asked.

'Ghost watch,' said Adam. 'We thought we could sit up all night in the church to watch out for the ghost, and people could sponsor us. There'd have to be an adult there, of course, we know that. But it'd still be brill. And we could get some money to stop the church from falling down.'

I looked at the three young faces in front of me, each of which seemed to be filled with a mixture of excitement and fear at the prospect of a 'ghost watch'. For a few seconds I was lost for words. When I finally spoke it was to attempt a combination of shared enthusiasm and considered prudence.

'You know there may not *be* a ghost,' I said tentatively. I felt a bit as if I were telling them that there was no Father Christmas.

'Course we do,' said Edwin, somewhat indignantly.

'I wouldn't mind betting they'd prefer it if there *wasn't* a ghost!' said Jack, grinning broadly.

The three scouts looked hurt at this, and Jack felt obliged to add a comment to the effect that he didn't mean it, and that he'd never come across a more intrepid threesome.

'I have to say,' I added, 'that there's another factor which may be a bit more immediate than the question of whether there's really a ghost or not. The fact is that you were just about the last people to see inside St

91

Mary's. I don't know if you realized, but the church was closed only a day or two after I showed you around. In some ways I think your idea is great. But I very much doubt that you'll be able to go into the church in broad daylight, let alone at night.'

'That's all right,' said Adam matter-of-factly. 'We didn't want to do anything during the summer hols, did we? And, anyway, according to the story, the ghost only walks about on the eve of All Hallows.'

'That's Halloween,' said Edwin helpfully.

'So we've got a few months yet,' said Gemma. 'Surely the church will be open by then.'

'Can we do it then?' asked Adam.

'Can we?' added Edwin. 'Please.'

I was rather taken aback by the completeness of the case that was being presented to me. I was also conscious that I could hardly sanction such an escapade without the support of Canon George. I had to assume, for the time being, that Jack would undertake to make arrangements for an adult presence at any night-time activity and see to it that all the parents were happy about the plan.

As I looked down at the eagerness and enthusiasm of the faces before me, I began to accuse myself for being so non-committal. If these scouts wanted to do it, then why shouldn't they? It surely wouldn't do any harm, and might even raise some money towards the church fund. There'd be little danger of the children being scared or worried by the experience if they were there as part of a supervised group in the church. It would just be a bit of fun.

'What do you think, Jack?' I asked.

'I've heard of worse schemes,' he said. 'I could sit up with them, of course, so it wouldn't be much different to when we're at camp. I can't say anyone gets a great deal of sleep on *those* occasions either. Speaking of which, you lot had better help get the last of that packing done before you scarper off home. Come on!'

'Does that mean we can do it?' said Adam.

'Can we?' added Edwin.

Gemma stayed quiet and looked at me intently.

'Look,' I said. 'I'm sorry, but I can't give you an answer just now. If we're talking about Halloween, then clearly it all depends on the church being open again. If it's *not* open, then I'm afraid I can't see how it could be done. If it *is* open . . . Well, then it will depend on a lot of things. Let me raise it with the vicar, then I can talk to you again when you're back from camp and when I get home from my holidays. OK? Let's leave it there for now. I'll do what I can. Now, come on, you get cracking with the rest of that camping kit – and I'll go home for my supper.'

Adam and Edwin each gave me one last pleading look before heading back to where Don and some of the other scouts were still sorting the ground sheets. Gemma moved indecisively, but then stayed in her seat.

'Can I please stay and talk to Michael for a bit?' she said to Jack, as he stood up. 'I just want to ask him something. That is, if he doesn't mind.'

Jack looked across to me for some indication of my willingness to stay.

'It's fine by me, Jack. If I can do or say anything to help Gemma, then that's what I'm here for.'

Jack looked enquiringly at his most energetic girl scout and then moved away, leaving me and Gemma sitting awkwardly alone in the corner of the church hall. I glanced at my watch as subtly as I could and wondered what Gemma could want to talk to me about.

'So, then, Gemma. What can I do for you?'

'It's about Izzy,' said Gemma quickly. There was a brief pause while I put the pieces together in my mind. The only Izzy I knew was Izzy Hutchings. How did Gemma know Izzy? Izzy Hutchings was the elderly woman who lived in Gracewell Court opposite the church. And then I remembered. On the day of the parish Summer Fayre, I had asked Adam, Edwin and Gemma to help Colin with the bunting. Gemma would have met Izzy whilst they were fixing the bunting between the church tower and the building opposite.

Gemma's next words to me confirmed the connection.

'You know the old lady in the flats over the road?' she said, flinging out an arm in the general direction of Gracewell Court. 'Well, me and the boys met her when we went over there to do those flags. I went into her flat and leaned out of the window with Edwin holding my legs while Adam threw the end of the rope up. He had to do it loads of times before I could catch it.'

She paused as if trying to recollect what had happened next.

'And that's when you met Izzy,' I said, prompting gently.

'Yeah. That's when I met her. I stayed there longer than the others because I wanted to put a sign on the flags, and I had some paper and pens with me so I could do it. Adam and Edwin went back down to do wet-sponge throwing and I stayed in the flat doing the sign. And Izzy gave me a glass of orange juice and three biscuits.'

'Well, that was very nice, Gemma. Did you talk much to Izzy?'

'Yeah, I did a bit. Although *she* talked most. All about people I hadn't heard of to begin with. Someone called

Wilson and someone called Foot. I think they were something to do with politics a long time ago. I don't know really. But then, after she talked about them, she talked about when she was my age. Fourteen. It was in the roaring twenties, she said. I'm not sure what was roaring about them. I think it was the nineteen twenties. It was really interesting. How she used to dance all the time. All the time, she said. Dancing. Dancing everywhere. At school and at home. And when she went out.

'She told me about how she used to float. I don't think she meant *really*. You know, I don't think she *really* floated. But she felt like she did. And she said she felt so free and happy. And then she started on about politics again. Somebody called Old MacDonald, or something like that. And then more about dancing. It was really good. Listening to her, I mean. Really interesting.'

I sat quietly, no longer inclined to look at my watch, but fascinated by the outpourings of a young girl who had been captivated by a woman nearly seventy years her senior. The quietness of our corner was regularly shattered by rumbling noises and thuds from the rest of the scouts at the other end of the hall, but Gemma seemed not to notice.

'Go on,' I said softly. Gemma's eyes seemed to be focused on a point about halfway down my chest, or perhaps on nothing at all.

'All the time I was drawing my sign,' continued Gemma, 'Izzy kept telling me about how free she had been when she was young. And then, when I had finished, she told me about being old.'

Gemma suddenly looked up at me and I could see the seeds of tears forming in the corners of her eyes.

'She said she didn't feel free any more. That she

hadn't done for a long time. She wasn't miserable about it. She kept laughing and saying you mustn't complain. That's what made it so sad. Because she wasn't moaning about it. She was just telling me because she wanted to tell someone, and I was the one who was there. And I thought it was so sad. She said sometimes it was like being a prisoner. She told me that one day she couldn't breathe properly and she had to get help. She said she couldn't call out because she couldn't breathe. So she had to bang on the wall. That wore her out even more and she fell down. But then her next door neighbour came in, and *she* knew what to do. Her name's Josie and she's a nurse.'

By now Gemma was sobbing silently, her young shoulders jerking involuntarily. I wanted to cuddle her, but felt acutely conscious that I was a man in a position of responsibility and she a young girl in my company. It seemed as if we were alone in our shared vulnerability, and that the heavy movements of the scouts at the end of the hall were really a universe away.

I reached out an arm and touched Gemma briefly but reassuringly on the arm. It seemed an awfully small contact in the face of the big world that she was growing up to know.

'Are you upset that Izzy is old?' I said, sensing immediately that it was not a good question to have asked.

Gemma looked up at me with the ghost of a smile around her lips, as if conscious of my own feeling of awkwardness.

'I think I'm upset because I know it's such a little thing to help someone like Izzy. And yet there must be so many people like her. And so many people who could help them, but who don't.'

'You could go and see her again,' I said.

Gemma smiled again.

'That's what I've been doing. I've been twice since the first time. That's how I know. When I'm there, Izzy tells me that she doesn't feel like a prisoner so much. And then she can talk to me about all those times when she used to dance. I suppose it's because she's old, and I'm young, do you think?'

Gemma was looking to me for advice, but I felt unable to give any. In the last few minutes I had learned much more from Gemma than she could have learned from anything I might have been able to say. I left the question dangling in the air and felt I wanted to cuddle her even more. Not as a comfort for her, but as a sign of love and appreciation. Appreciation for what her own unpretentious love had already brought into Izzy's life, and for what it was now bringing into mine.

This time, however, I did not even place a hand on her arm. I suppose I was frightened of compromising her innocence – and mine. I fought back the tears that were welling behind my own eyes and smiled at her.

'And what was it you wanted to ask me?' I said.

'Oh, I didn't want to ask you anything really,' she replied. 'I just wanted to tell you what was in my head. Like Izzy tells *me* what's in *hers*. I feel better now. Thanks very much.'

And, with no more than a quick smile, Gemma rose and returned to her friends who, by now, were nearing the end of their evening's work.

I watched her move away, imagining that I saw in her what Amy might be in less than ten years' time. I stood up and, with a last wave to Jack, Don and the rest of the boys and girls, left the church hall to walk home. As I passed by the church I looked up at Gracewell Court, where I could see a light shining brightly in Izzy's window.

Commitments at work were such that it was a few days before I was back on church property again. I returned to the vicarage for a meeting of the group that was overseeing the fund-raising schemes for the repairs to St Mary's. Hilary Noble was there as parish secretary. Frank Foster was there as churchwarden of St Mary's. So too was Alan Watts, churchwarden of St John's, as it had been agreed that any fund-raising should be a parish concern and not simply a matter for the congregation of St Mary's. Alan also had the role of acting parish treasurer and, with his sometimes frightening efficiency, was better equipped than anyone to oversee the various fund-raising events. The other people at the meeting were Lynda Soames, whose Outreach Group had been well to the fore in organizing activities of one kind or another, and Canon George.

The first hour or so was taken up with a review of the various events that had already taken place since the end of May. There had been a mini-market, a jumble sale, a 'bring-and-buy', a 'nearly-new', two coffee mornings, a recital, a sponsored walk, a sponsored sing, a flower show, a junior disco, and, of course, the Summer Fayre. In addition, there had been a significant level of extra giving, including two large anonymous donations. All in all the parish had already worked tremendously hard to do everything possible to raise money. Indeed, in a period of no more than three months, a sum of nearly ten thousand pounds had been raised and, with more activities to come following the summer break, the group was feeling justifiably pleased with progress to date.

'I have to say at once,' said Canon George as soon as Alan had completed the review, 'Praise the Lord! For he has come to our aid at this time of crisis. We were feeling beaten by the waves and the wind was against us. But he has come to us, walking on the sea of our faith, to deliver us from the storm. Praise the Lord!'

'Amen to that,' said Frank.

'Alleluia!' almost sang Lynda.

'And even more to come,' added Alan, whose mind was still filled with pounds rather than praises. 'My planning network for the period from September to the end of the year already shows an average of two things a week. Some of them are quite small scale. For example, Joy Bartholomew is offering to provide copies of her recipe for green tomato chutney at ten pence each.'

'How nice,' said Hilary, embarrassed by the silence that had greeted the news.

'Have you tasted it?' asked Frank, with a look that implied some terrible suffering on a previous occasion. He added curtly that he for one would feel more inclined to part with his money if Joy promised never to make any green tomato chutney ever again.

'There are also a few larger scale activities,' continued Alan. 'Key among them, of course, will be the Harvest Supper which this year will include some cabaret items from amongst our ranks. We thought we would call it "Hidden Talents".'

My reaction to the idea of such a cabaret was that people should perhaps be sponsored *not* to reveal their hidden talents.

'Whilst I can sympathize to some extent with that sentiment, Michael,' said Canon George, 'I feel we would disappoint a lot of people if we adopted that view. I know that Christine has been practising her juggling. And John and Rose Burgess are preparing an Egyptian dance.'

Church people can be terribly polite when they want to be. Where this last announcement from the vicar might have brought forth a guffaw, titter, or even an exclamation like 'What the . . .!', it drew forth no more than a series of serious nods from Frank, Alan and Hilary. Had Stephen Pickle been here, I reflected, he would by now have been stuffing a handkerchief in his mouth.

'And people are going to *pay* to witness this?' I said, my voice quivering just the slightest amount.

'Indeed they are,' interjected Alan. 'There will be an entrance fee, and then folk will be invited to contribute more if they like the acts.'

'If they are entranced, you mean,' said Frank, grinning.

'I'm sorry?' said Alan.

'Entranced,' said Frank again. 'Entrance fee. Entranced. It's a joke.'

'Oh,' said Alan, who did not share Frank's sense of humour.

'If I may,' I said, 'I'd like to add another scheme to your list, Alan.'

I then outlined as briefly as I could the idea that had been put to me a few days before by Adam, Edwin and Gemma. I related the story of the ghost and how it had captured their imaginations. I explained how exactly I thought the 'ghost watch' might work – how one of the scout leaders or I would stay up with the small band of children to make sure that they came to no harm, how the scouts had felt that they could raise a fair bit of money through sponsorship. And how the preferred date for this 'little enterprise' was Halloween, which this year fell on a Saturday.

I was listened to in complete silence – a sign which I took to be either very supportive or very ominous. It wasn't long before I realized which.

Whilst I outlined my plan for a series of night-time activities to keep the scouts busy in the church, Lynda stared at me, her eyes widening in apparent disbelief and her mouth dropping open as if not sure what she should say. Finally she found her voice.

'You cannot be serious,' she said. 'Michael, tell me you're not serious. Canon George?'

She looked at the vicar for some endorsement of her shock, but Canon George clearly wanted to hear more from both of us before intervening.

I was rather confused. I hadn't discussed the idea with anyone, but it had never for one moment occurred to me that there might be any real objection to it. I had foreseen some issues, like discussing the details for how the parents would be approached, and what sorts of guarantees we would be able to provide as far as food, bedding and supervision were concerned. Naïvely, perhaps, I had assumed that the parish would be generally appreciative of anything that raised more money for the church and which involved young people in some active way.

'I'm sorry,' I said, looking from one face to another and trying to find a degree of support, no matter how small. 'But why should there be a problem? These are children who would never normally ask to come into our church. I'd make sure that they were well looked after.'

'Well looked after!' said Lynda, who was trying to keep her mixture of surprise and anger under control. 'Do you honestly realize what you are suggesting?'

I must have looked as if I wouldn't or couldn't answer, because she went on.

'You, a clergyman, talking about ghosts. On Halloween of all nights. And if that wasn't bad enough on its own, to involve children. To actually encourage them to think they might be part of this . . . this . . . work of the devil. And in our church building as well. I'm almost lost for words!'

As she stopped there was an awful silence. All that could be heard was the sound of breathing. I looked around, but the others were mainly looking at their shoes or at their knees. Lynda was wringing her hands together and clearly trying to calm herself. Canon George judged that now was the time for him to speak.

'I think we should try to understand each other's point of view here,' he said, so slowly and quietly that it was almost a whisper. No one else said anything. 'Michael first mentioned the story of the ghost to me some weeks ago. I'd come across something like it when I arrived in the parish, but had heard nothing about it since. On the whole I am inclined to believe that the story of the vagrant is something of a local legend, with little basis in fact. If I really believed St Mary's to be haunted by a ghost, I would have done something about it years ago.' Canon George looked around the room, but still no one else felt inclined to speak.

'I have to believe,' he continued, 'that Michael's motivation in this matter is an innocent one. The motivation of wanting to encourage the children in a scheme which they had dreamed up themselves. The motivation of wanting to involve them in something to do with the church and the campaign to save it. Is that right, Michael?'

I simply said, 'Yes', and tried not to look at Lynda.

'Lynda's objection,' continued the vicar, 'if I understand it correctly, is to the fact that, through this particular event, the children are being encouraged in their belief about ghosts. That they risk approaching the spiritual world through something which is dark rather than through something which is light.'

Canon George was clearly trying to pick his way through the issues like a man walking on tiptoe through a minefield. He looked to Lynda for a reaction. She nodded fitfully, showing some agreement to his thesis, but betraying her feeling that his words stopped short of reflecting the strength of her feelings about ghosts and Halloween.

'How would you both – how would everyone else – feel if we thought of the whole thing in a different way?' Canon George smiled that calm smile of his before continuing. 'Michael doesn't want to lose this chance to encourage and involve the scouts, I'm sure. Lynda is concerned that they might come under evil influences. Could we perhaps not simply reposition the idea as a sponsored "watch"? After all, we have "watches" in the church at other times during the Christian year. Don't you think, Lynda, that the children just *might* be open to the influence of the Holy Spirit by being in the church with Michael?'

Lynda pushed back her long hair and exhaled loudly down her nose.

'That's all very well,' she said, her voice trembling slightly, 'but, if you'll excuse me, you know full well that, as far as the children are concerned, they will still think they're there to look out for a ghost. And what happens if the local press get to hear of it?'

Canon George paused to think of the consequences to which Lynda had alluded, and then he looked at me.

'Michael,' he said. 'You don't believe in this ghost story, do you?'

'I don't think so,' I said. And then, aware that perhaps I should be sounding rather more definite, 'No. No, I don't.'

'Well, do you think that you could support the scouts in a sponsored night-time exercise, whilst also encouraging them away from a belief in a questionable ghost story and towards an encounter with the Holy Spirit?'

I said 'Yes', but felt unsure. Logically I knew that he was right. Perhaps also that Lynda was right. But, even so, I felt as if I were letting them down. As if I risked transforming the scouts and their adventure into something more like a Sunday School outing.

'You could perhaps see it as a way of setting them free from a very limited view of what is spiritual, and opening them up to an *unlimited* one.'

Again, my lack of enthusiasm must have been only too obvious, but I nodded and said 'Yes' once more.

'Does that mean the thing is going ahead?' said Alan, who was the first of the others to speak.

'I think, for the time being,' said Canon George, 'we have to leave that decision with Michael. He's heard Lynda's objections. In a matter so touching upon the world of the spirit, I think we should all leave some space for reflection. Space for the Holy Spirit to move and guide us in this matter. What does everyone else think?'

I'm not sure what everyone else thought. Faced with the transformation of 'a bit of fun' into a traumatic decision, my mind sought escape in thoughts of the family holiday that would begin in two days' time, and which would whisk me away from the worries of the parish – at least for two weeks.

With the scouts already at summer camp, I decided that any further thought about the 'watch' – ghost or otherwise – would have to wait. Who knows, I thought? Perhaps they'll go off the idea.

SEVEN

How to Spell

*'You will know the truth, and the truth will
make you free.'* John 8:32

It seemed that no sooner had we arrived back from
holiday than it was time for Amy to start school again.
It was the beginning of her second year in the infants,
and nearly time for her sixth birthday. Cheryl and I had
met Amy's new teacher, Miss Simcox, at the end of the
previous term, and she had told us of her plans to bring
the parents more into the life of the class. One of her
ideas involved asking some of the parents to come in
during the day to talk to the class about things they did
whilst the children were at school. She had already
lined up Beatrice's mother to talk about looking after a
baby – Beatrice's small sister, Eleanor. One of the
fathers had been approached to talk about his sweet
shop. All the children were hoping that he would
arrive with free samples. And yes, you guessed it,
yours truly had volunteered his services as well.

When Amy first heard about this she was less than
fully enthusiastic.

'You're not going to wear that silly thing round your
neck, are you?'

When I assured her that I would not be wearing the
silly thing round my neck, her attitude softened.

'I don't mind too much when you *talk* about vicars,
but I don't want you to *look* like one.'

'Fine,' I said flatly. If this was the way she talked to
me as she approached her sixth birthday, I couldn't

help thinking that it was likely to be uphill from here on.

'You can talk about adverts, I think,' she said seriously, as if she were giving me my brief.

'Thanks very much,' I said.

Here I was, giving up valuable time at work to be with my daughter and her friends, and being treated with less consideration than I might have expected from a conference of frozen pizza salesmen.

When I arrived at South House School on the designated afternoon in early September, Miss Simcox was waiting for me with the kind of smile that I imagine the Emperor Nero must have had on his face as he watched the first Christians led out to face the lions.

'Mr Dunn,' she said in that inimitable way of hers that made my name sound like a death knell. 'Mr Dunn, how good of you to come. The children are waiting eagerly for you.'

'Ready for the prey, eh, Miss Simcox?'

Miss Simcox looked at me oddly, her large and threatening teeth bared in a smile of embarrassment.

'Well,' she said, 'I'm not sure they're actually *ready* to pray. But you can try if you like.'

'No,' I stammered. 'What I meant was . . .' But the moment had passed, and Miss Simcox was already striding purposefully towards the classroom.

'This is Mr Dunn,' she said to the assembled class once we had entered the room. The faces of the children conveyed the whole range of expressions from complete vacancy to rapturous and unnatural interest. I could see that Amy had not yet decided whether to own up to me, although a couple of friends were jabbing her in the ribs and saying things like 'Is he yours, then?' If her eyes conveyed anything at all, it was the single thought 'This had better be good'.

I sat down on a tiny chair that Miss Simcox had thoughtfully placed for me and began by saying hello and asking who watched television. After a unified show of hands (during which Miss Simcox leaned across to whisper in my ear that she sincerely hoped the children looked at some books as well), I started asking them which TV adverts they liked most. From there I progressed to telling them something about how their favourite adverts were made.

It was quite an interactive session, with many of the children joining in and asking questions, and I soon found that I was enjoying myself. After about twenty minutes, Miss Simcox stood up and told the children that they would have to release Mr Dunn soon so that he could go back to making more adverts.

It was then that Beatrice asked her question.

'What about your *other* job?' she said. 'Are you going to tell us about your other job?'

Miss Simcox sat down again and once more leaned across with a whisper. 'Beatrice is referring to your vicaring,' she said, clearly under the impression that I might have forgotten what my other job was.

While I felt Miss Simcox's sibilant words sliding into my right ear, I glanced across at Amy who was giving Beatrice one of her most withering looks. It was a look that seemed to say 'Call yourself my best friend, do you! Fancy you going and asking about my dad's other job when you know full well that it's the most embarrassing thing in the world!'

Miss Simcox must have seen the way I was looking at Amy, because her next words were designed to bring my daughter into the conversation.

'Well, Amy,' she said. 'Perhaps *you* would like to tell us about your father's other job.'

Amy screwed her face up into an expression of

intense thought and then said quickly, 'He does magic.'

There was a brief pause whilst Miss Simcox looked at me and I looked at Amy and Amy looked at Beatrice.

Those children who did not count among Amy's best friends, and who did not know that I was a clergyman, all suddenly started to look interested again. One young chap put up his hand.

'Yes, Douglas,' said Miss Simcox.

'Can Mr Dung show us some magic, please, Miss?'

I squirmed uncomfortably in my seat and tried to make eye contact with Amy.

'I'm afraid I don't really do magic,' I said at last, fearing a wave of recrimination and disappointment.

'Yes, he does,' said Amy quickly. 'Well, not now he doesn't. But he's learning to.'

Once again I looked at Amy disbelievingly and shook my head slowly from side to side. What on earth was she thinking about?

'He's learning,' she said again. 'He's learning to change things.'

Everyone, adult and child alike, was now looking at Amy.

'He's learning to change water into wine,' she said.

Miss Simcox's mouth dropped open at this point.

'No, that's not right,' continued Amy. 'He's not learning to change water into wine. He's learning to change wine into something. I've forgotten. Somebody's blood, I think.'

A few of the boys looked at each other menacingly. Some of the girls simultaneously burst into an elongated 'Yeeeeuuuch!' Others simply looked terrified. 'Blood!' said Douglas excitedly, his estimation of 'Mr Dung' clearly rising as he pictured me as some kind of vampire.

Amy hadn't finished.

'My dad said it's like doing the magic,' she said. 'Changing those things. Whatever they are. I think he casts a spell on them.'

Next to me Miss Simcox spluttered. I held my head in my hands. I remembered how, when Amy had once seen me practising my movements for the Eucharist in preparation for my ordination to the priesthood, she had asked me what I was doing. Not wanting to go into any details, I simply said it was like 'doing the magic'. The words had obviously stuck in her memory. Here I was, only a month away from my first Eucharist as a priest, and the news in the playground and at the school gate would be all about how the honorary curate was indulging in magic.

Miss Simcox, regaining her composure, obviously decided that enough damage had been done talking about my 'other job'. With a determined air, she strove to move the discussion back on to safer territory.

'Let's leave the magic, shall we? I'm sure you would all like to ask Mr Dunn about something else to do with his advertising job.'

For the most part, the children looked as if they would rather have stayed on the subject of magical transformations, but Douglas came to the aid of Miss Simcox by holding up his hand once more.

'Yes, Douglas?' said Miss Simcox.

'I want to ask Mr Dung if you have to know how to spell to do the adverts. 'Cos my dad says a lot of them are stupid.'

Miss Simcox's lips were once more at my ear.

'We were doing some spelling before you arrived,' she whispered, clearly feeling that Douglas's comment needed some explanation. 'Douglas isn't very keen on spelling.'

I nodded at Miss Simcox, and looked back at Douglas.

'Learning how to spell is useful for most things,' I said, trying to win back a bit of Miss Simcox's sympathy.

'Amen,' she whispered once more with a chuckle, before adding 'just a little joke'.

* * *

'You said *what*?' said Cheryl later that afternoon when we were discussing the references to 'magic'.

'It wasn't me,' I said in my best exasperated tone. 'It was that daughter of yours. She was the one who brought it up!'

'But she was only repeating what she heard you say,' said Cheryl, burying herself once more in a pile of books. The new term at college was still another week away, and she was making changes to some of her lectures. I looked hurt and drank my tea.

'As it happens,' she continued after a pause, 'I don't think "magic" is such a bad word to use anyway.'

I must have looked puzzled as I chewed thoughtfully on a digestive biscuit.

'I don't mean "magic" in the traditional sense, of course,' Cheryl went on. 'Not party tricks. But something powerful. When you think about it the power of transformation is a bit mysterious, after all. A bit magical really.'

'Transformation?'

'Yes, you know. What you're all about as a church minister. What we're *all* about as Christians. What was it you were saying several months back? Setting people free?'

I put down my cup and saucer and settled back on the sofa. Upstairs I could hear Amy moving about. Considering her small size, it sounded as if she were teaching a baby elephant to clog dance.

110

'What's transformation got to do with setting people free? And where does the magic come in?' I asked.

Cheryl pushed her hair out of her eyes and looked thoughtful.

'I'm not really sure,' she said. 'It just feels all of a piece, that's all. I know magic's not the right word, but in a way it sums up something that's a bit beyond our understanding. Most transformations are like that. Things that we might believe in rationally, but which are still somehow a bit, well, "magic". Like a caterpillar changing into a butterfly or a seed becoming a flower.'

'I still don't see what that has to do with setting people free,' I said, slipping off my shoes and putting my feet on a cushion.

'I suppose I mean something about helping people to become what God wants them to be. Isn't that what you meant when you talked about setting people free?'

I moved my head about in a generally supportive way as I thought back over the various comments I had made to Cheryl on this subject.

'Possibly,' I said, conscious that I wasn't at all sure what I had meant.

'Well, perhaps that's where the magic comes in,' Cheryl said. 'The thing that transforms the caterpillar into the butterfly.'

'That's nature,' I said.

'Or God,' said Cheryl. 'That's what makes it so interesting, I think. The same letters that spell "nature" for one person spell "God" for someone else. Or even "magic".'

Cheryl looked down at her books and I stared at the ceiling, letting her words flow back and forth in my mind for a minute or two. Finally those thoughts led me back to my experience at South House School earlier that afternoon.

'Talking of spelling, I think I'd rather bear the brunt of Philip's wrath any day than have to learn spelling from Miss Simcox.'

Cheryl suddenly sat bolt upright.

'Oh!' she exclaimed. 'Philip. Philip your boss. He rang while you were at the school and asked if you could call him back as soon as possible. Oh, I'm sorry, darling. I forgot!'

I jumped off the sofa and growled at Cheryl as I made my way out to the phone in the kitchen. Philip had said nothing to me when I booked the afternoon as a half-day holiday, but I knew that my occasional absences from work were a source of some irritation. At least, I reflected, this particular absence had not been the result of my church duties in the parish.

The phone seemed to ring for ages before I heard Philip's voice.

'Ah, Michael. Thanks for ringing back. I thought you'd want to hear that we've just been approached by Crombie Computers who'd like us to handle their business. It could be worth about four million pounds this year.'

'But we haven't pitched for the Crombie business, have we? Why did they choose us?'

Philip laughed. It was such an unusual sound that I nearly fell off the stool on which I was perching.

'Well, Michael, that's the funny thing – and why I wanted you to be the first to hear. They'd apparently had a bad experience with their last agency. You know, I reckon the Crombie Marketing Director is a very insecure guy. Anyway, he says he couldn't trust any one of them. Which is where *you* came in.'

'I don't understand,' I said weakly.

'He'd apparently met Mulligan from Pronto Pizzas at one of those Marketing Society bashes, and Mulligan suggested he came to us on the strength of you. He said that as you were a vicar you were probably the straightest advertising guy around. Which is just the sort of thing the chaps at Crombies wanted to hear. So well done! Well done for doing nothing – except somehow winning us the business! And now, as they say, you're on the case!'

I started muttering something about being pleased that the agency had finally secured a big account in the computer industry but Philip cut me off with, 'OK, well, we'll talk about it tomorrow. You go and pour yourself a drink. You deserve it. And, by the way, don't think of today as a holiday. Consider it a day working at home.'

He laughed again.

'And we'll have to think how we can play that "vicar" card again, I reckon. If it's likely to win us business, we'd better make a lot more noise about your vocation! See you tomorrow.'

I wandered back into the drawing room and the enquiring face of Cheryl.

'Good or bad news?' she asked.

'I'm not sure,' I said truthfully. 'I'm really not sure.'

* * *

The novelty of being at home during a day when Cheryl was not at work meant that, for a few hours at least, there was a semblance of real family life in the Dunn residence. Cheryl and I had a light meal with Amy soon after six o'clock, and then I read my daughter a story. I decided not to raise again with her the subject of the afternoon visit to her class, and *her* only comment on the incident was that everyone liked me. Oh well, I thought, it couldn't have been *that* bad.

It was then bath-time and by eight o'clock she was

ready for bed. I bid her goodnight and left her listening to a taped recording of some children's poems. Downstairs Cheryl had finished working for the day and was curled up on a pile of cushions watching a soap opera.

'I know you hate it,' she said, referring to what was on the TV, 'but it means I don't have to think – and I need *some* kind of release after revising all those lectures. Isn't there some poor unsuspecting parishioner you should be visiting?'

I bent down to kiss her.

'You've just given me an idea,' I said. 'But I'd better make a call first to see if he's there.'

Cheryl looked quizzical.

'Peter,' I said. 'Peter Strang. The carpenter.'

Peter *was* there, and happy to see me at such short notice. I should find him in the workshop, he said. I told Cheryl that I would be out for only an hour or so, and set off for Peter's workshop straightaway. Twenty minutes later I entered the alley and at the end of the small terrace, I turned into Peter's garden and made my way to the workshop at the back.

The sky was overcast and it was beginning to get dark. The garden had a more ghostly feel about it than when I had been there the first time, probably because it seemed so much quieter. No longer full of the sunshine and hum of early summer, the garden was now cloaked in shadow, with the only light coming from the windows of the workshop itself. I knocked lightly on the door and the familiar deep voice bade me enter.

Inside the workshop everything seemed transfigured from how I had remembered it. Where before the space had been brimmed with a soft orange glow, it was now picked out in sharp contrasts of light and shade by the white bulb which hung from the ceiling.

In this light Peter's face seemed etched with lines as

he rose from his place to greet me with a warm hand-shake and the sort of smile that set his blue eyes twinkling below his tanned forehead.

'I'm sorry to disturb you,' I said, sitting down heavily on the chair he pulled out for me. 'It's good of you to let me come round.'

'Good?' he said ruminatively, before adding, 'You can come any time. I'm here mostly.'

I smiled back and we sat in perfect silence for a few seconds. I had already learned that Peter only spoke when he had something to say, and I tried hard not to slip into the trivia of small talk. Even so it was something of a relief when the short silence was ended by Peter saying, 'Would you like something to drink?'

I looked around and could see no sign of a kettle or mugs. If the offer of a drink meant moving back into the house, I should decline it. There was something about the atmosphere of the workshop which I valued and, even though I had no knowledge of what Peter's cottage was like, I felt that it was unlikely to offer quite the tranquillity of this place. My hesitation must have shown, for Peter spoke again.

'There's not much of a choice. Just malt whisky.'

He smiled at me, before opening a cabinet to his left and taking out a half-full bottle of Glenlivet.

I smiled back.

'That sounds like a great idea,' I said, genuinely pleased at this show of warmth and hospitality. 'Yes, please.'

Peter took from the cabinet two small glasses that looked very old and almost filled them with generous helpings of the malt whisky.

'One of my weaknesses, I'm afraid,' said Peter, managing to look bashful and self-confident at the same time. 'Don't tell anyone, but I get a lot of it for free. I've a nephew who works for a distributor. He doesn't like whisky and passes his freebies on to me.'

I was grateful for the shared confidence and the relaxed air that seemed to have settled on our conversation.

'Talking of free Scotch . . .' I began, only to let the words fade on my lips.

Peter looked up at me.

'Nothing,' I muttered. 'Nothing.' And then, 'This is very good. Thanks very much. Cheers.'

'Good health,' said Peter.

We relished our whisky in silence for a second or two, and then Peter began to speak again.

'You'll want to see the stool.'

'Well,' I replied, 'it would be good to see how far you've got with it.'

'It's finished,' said Peter.

I must have looked surprised. After my first visit to his workshop, he had left a more detailed design for me at church. I had confirmed the commission over the telephone, and then largely forgotten about it. Somehow I had assumed that, even with only four weeks to go to the due date, the stool would not yet be finished.

'I made a few changes to the original design,' said Peter. 'I hope you like it. If you don't, I can find another use for it. So say what you think.'

'Like it? I'm sure I'll love it,' I exclaimed. Not being a practical person, I was always in awe of people who could make things with their hands. I had no doubts that I would love whatever Peter had decided to make of the stool.

He stood up and walked to the back of the workshop which was dark in shadow. He bent down and then turned around, holding in his arms an object which was still shrouded with a gabardine cloth. He set the object on the bench next to where I was sitting, and then without ceremony removed the cloth.

I gasped and put down my glass with a heavy thud. This was not just a stool. It was a work of art. There standing in front of me was a most beautiful piece of furniture, sculpted in oak. The seat was curved and delicately shaped, with a Celtic cross design carved into the surface. The four legs were not simply functional. They were also patterned with Celtic art, each one seeming to vibrate with life.

'It's . . . it's . . . stunning,' I said at last. 'Absolutely stunning. You're a genius!'

I smiled broadly at Peter and held out my hand to shake his. He looked at me in a way that conveyed a hint of pride, but mainly embarrassment.

'Not a genius. No,' he said gently. 'Certainly not that.'

I had begun to run my fingers over the wood of the stool, and to feel the shape and the patterns coming alive beneath their touch.

Peter refilled our glasses and, seeing my absorption, began to speak more freely than I had heard him before.

'When I was at school, a long time ago,' he began, 'I had trouble with words. I found it difficult to write properly, and I never really knew how to spell. I still don't, I'm afraid.'

I didn't want Peter to stop talking, so I glanced at him briefly and then returned to the stool, feeling that he would be more relaxed with my attention focused on the wood rather than on his words.

'When I started doing woodwork,' he continued, 'I found another language. It's a way of letting the ghost out!'

He laughed, and I stopped caressing the wood to look at him.

'Letting the ghost out?' I said.

'Just an expression,' said Peter. 'Just words. Something my old teacher used to say. He was a clergyman, you see. Not like you, of course. He was the old school. He used to quote a bit from the Communion service, in the old prayer book. A bit where it said if anyone needed comfort they should go to a clergyman to receive the benefit of ghostly counsel and advice. That's what he said. I'll always remember it. Ghostly counsel and advice. He said that everyone had a ghost in them. I suppose he meant a spirit. But "ghost" was the word he used. And he said that what we had to do was find a way in which the ghost could be let out.'

'And *your* ghost is let out through your work with wood? Is that what you mean, Peter?'

'Something like that.' He took a large swig of the whisky and settled himself on his chair. 'As you can see, I can let a lot out once the spirit is in me!'

I took a drink and waited to see if he would go on. He rubbed his chin thoughtfully and reached out to touch the leg of the stool before resuming.

'Yes. It lets the ghost out of me,' he said. 'And I think it lets the ghost out of the wood as well. That probably doesn't make any sense. I don't always make sense. But perhaps you'll understand more than most.'

I reached out to touch the stool myself. I was touched by his faith in me.

'You see,' he went on, 'I sometimes think that when the wood is changed into the stool, or whatever it is I'm making, then it's really as if I'm letting the ghost out of the wood. So that the wood always had the stool in it, but that it needed help to get out. Do you see what I mean? In a way, I just set the stool free from the wood. I release it to be a stool rather than just a piece of wood.'

Peter stopped suddenly and laughed again.

'I don't know,' he chuckled. 'I really do talk some rubbish when I've had a glass of this.'

I didn't smile back.

'I don't think it's rubbish,' I said. 'I think it's very spiritual.'

Peter looked into his glass.

'I remember,' I continued, 'that when we first met, you told me that you didn't go to church. But, if I may say so, there is something very spiritual about what you do. Do you believe in God?'

I was not trying to engage in some doorstep evangelism. I was trying to learn from the man who was sitting a few feet away from me.

Fortunately Peter responded to my question in the spirit in which it was intended.

'I believe in *something*,' he said softly. 'I don't think it's what I was taught to believe in when I was a child. I think it's something I've only really learned about as I grew older. You see, I think there's more to what I do than simply shaping wood. My skill, if you like, can make a stool. That's a natural talent I've been lucky enough to develop. But if you see more in it than just a stool, then that's because there's been something added. Something from somewhere else. Something that's come from more than my natural skill. Something *super*natural, I suppose. Something that's out there,' he gestured vaguely at the ceiling of the workshop, 'but something that's in here as well,' he struck himself on the chest. 'That's the ghost, I suppose. It's out there, and it's in here. And if that's what you call God, then fine. But it's not something I felt when I used to go to church. So I stopped going. Because I can find more of it here.'

He stopped and put down his glass.

'I'm sorry,' he continued, 'I've said too much. You came here for a stool, not a sermon. And that's the truth.'

I wanted to say something from the heart, but was conscious I might sound glib.

'The stool is that much more beautiful for what you have just told me,' I said. 'I'll treasure it that much more for knowing what I know now.'

Peter looked pleased by the comment and offered me another drink.

'No thanks,' I said. 'I'd better get back. Although we still need to discuss a price.'

'Not yet,' said Peter, holding up his hand. 'We still don't know if it's good.'

'If it's good?' I said. 'It's not only good. It's great!'

'No. That's not what I mean. We'll only know if it's good if it serves its purpose. As a stool. It's a stool now before it's anything else. You need to use it as a stool to know if it's good.'

'OK,' I said, giving in. 'But that means *you*'ll need to see it used as well. You'll have to be there. Even though you don't go to church, you'll have to be there. At my first Eucharist.'

Peter stood up. The meeting was over.

'I'll come to see if the stool is good,' he said with a smile. 'But only if you accept it as a gift.'

The words formed on my lips to argue with him, but I could see from the expression on his face that there was no point. He had made up his mind on the matter. There was no way that he was going to let me pay for the stool.

'I accept,' I said, taking his hand in mine. 'Thank you. Thank you very much indeed.'

I picked up the stool and prepared to leave. As I walked out through the garden I stopped to look back at where Peter stood in the workshop doorway, framed by the light. I turned again to leave the place and said a prayer of thanks – for Peter, for his work, and because I felt that I had learned something more about spirituality and how to set people free.

EIGHT

Hidden Talents

*'Do you not say, "Four months more, then
comes the harvest"?'* John 4:35

The church was due some good news, and the timing
of this particular bit of good news could not have been
better.

'St Mary's will be open in just under two weeks'
time,' said Canon George, his rubicund face displaying
one of the biggest smiles seen in the parish for a while.
'I'll be able to announce it at the Harvest Supper this
Saturday.'

Canon George put the ends of his fingers together,
exhaled deeply and cast his eyes heavenwards.
Stephen and I looked at each other.

'You're sure about this?' said Stephen tentatively,
knowing only too well that reports of the health of St
Mary's had been none too reliable in the past.

'I heard it from the diocesan surveyor's lips no more
than two hours ago when he telephoned me,' said
Canon George. 'There'll be a letter in the post tomorrow. The workmen have started dismantling the
scaffolding, but it will take all of this week and some of
next for them to finish. We'll then have to clean the
place up.'

'Which means it will all have taken about four
months,' I added, flicking through my diary and remembering the day when I first noticed the signs of
the crumbling stonework at the top of the pillars.

The three of us were meeting at the vicarage one midweek evening in September. Canon George had barely been able to wait until Stephen and I were seated before he told us the good news.

'So the trouble really wasn't that serious after all,' said Stephen, straightening his cassock and settling himself more comfortably on the sofa.

'Well, Stephen,' said Canon George, his brow furrowing slightly. 'It all depends what you mean by serious. We were indeed fortunate that the problem was not terminal as we were once inclined to believe. On the other hand, four months without St Mary's has clearly been a serious loss for many of our flock. Which is why I think it's important that we use the re-opening as the excuse for a celebration. A parish party. This is, after all, a rebirth, a real resurrection experience. St Mary's which once seemed lost is found again. And we must thank God for that in every way we know how. The Harvest Supper should be just the start. Having begun to gather in the gifts of our past and present, we must make sure we use them well in the future. And then there's Michael's ordination as priest. That's now only just over two weeks away, which means that Michael's first Eucharist can be at St Mary's after all.'

Since the beginning of summer Canon George and Stephen Pickle had been teaching me the theory and practice of the Eucharist in preparation for my priesting. Over the last few weeks in particular we had had several sessions together to work through the order of service itself. Most of this had been done at St John's, although we had spent one evening together in St Mary's when it became apparent that the remedial work was nearing completion.

'That,' said Canon George excitedly, 'will be a wonderful occasion for the parish. What better way to reopen a church than by bringing everyone together to celebrate a special calling within its midst. It will be like a new Pentecost.'

Canon George sighed again and the three of us sat in silence for a moment or two remembering that Pentecost had been something of a damp squib, coming so soon after the news of the problem at St Mary's.

'So much to look forward to,' said the vicar at last. 'And so much to plan. On which note we need to review the details for the Harvest Supper, the re-opening of St Mary's, and Michael's first Eucharist. Before we do that, are there any other forthcoming events that ought to be on our agenda?'

Stephen pushed out his bottom lip in a meditative manner and then shook his head slowly.

'Michael?' prompted Canon George.

I hesitated and then said, 'Well, there *is* the matter of the ghost watch at Halloween.'

I updated my two clergy colleagues on the position as it stood. That the scouts were still keen to do it. That objections had been raised by Lynda Soames on her own behalf, and subsequently on behalf of several other of the more evangelical members of the congregation. That I had had a private meeting with Lynda at her home at which I had suggested how I was extremely reluctant to disappoint the scouts, but that I hoped I could understand and respond to her position. That I might re-position the event, as had been suggested at the earlier meeting of the fund-raising group. That any explicit reference to 'ghosts' be avoided, but that an overnight watch go ahead under some other pretext.

Lynda had listened patiently to all that I said, but nevertheless restated her views on the matter. When we parted we were still divided. Almost the only good thing about the evening was that I had briefly met for the first time Lynda's husband, Gordon, who seemed a very amiable fellow.

'So what exactly does that mean?' asked Canon George at the end of my discursive narrative. 'Is this ghost watch – I mean this "watch" – going ahead or not?'

I looked at Stephen for some sign of approval or disapproval, but he simply shrugged his shoulders and pulled a face as if to say, 'Sorry, mate, but this is *your* call'.

I started slowly.

'I don't want to upset or provoke those who are against it,' I began. 'But, with St Mary's reopening, I feel we need to make the church building immediately inviting to those sorts of people who would not normally be part of it. Like the scouts. Had St Mary's still been closed at Halloween it would, of course, have made the whole thing so much simpler. But I really don't think I can dodge this one. The scouts came up with this idea as a way of contributing something to the cost of the work. I really do think it would be very mean-spirited of us – I mean of *me* – to say no now.'

There was a brief silence.

'I think you have to do what you feel is right,' said Canon George. 'I think that Stephen and I will support you in that.' He looked to Stephen and his curate nodded seriously.

'Right,' I said. And then, not knowing what else to say, 'Thank you.'

* * *

It was Saturday evening and the night of the parish Harvest Supper and 'Hidden Talents' show. The event was due to begin at seven, but by six o'clock St Mary's hall was already in a state of high drama.

'I've said it before and I'll say it again,' said Mary Brown, her lips pouting and her eyelashes fluttering. 'There really is only so much you can do with a quiche.' And with a haggard look of weary desperation she gazed down at a trestle table on which were no fewer than twenty-eight quiches of varying sizes and hues. 'Next time,' she continued with a look that suggested she for one might not survive *this* time, 'we'll ask people to specify what they're going to do. When we did one of these things a few years ago, you couldn't move for sausage rolls. Tonight we've got twelve sausage rolls between a hundred and sixty people, and enough quiches to feed the three thousand.'

'Five thousand, dear, five thousand,' prompted Mary West, 'or even four thousand. But almost certainly not three.'

'Well, whatever,' responded Mary Brown, somewhat aggrieved. 'All I know is, we're going to be very glad we've got Mrs Clubb's hotpot.'

'Not to mention your own meat loaf,' said Mary West.

'Well, I wasn't going to mention it,' said Mary Brown.

'Of course not, dear,' said Mary West.

The two Marys were, as you might have imagined, the prime movers in the organization of the Harvest Supper. Over a period of weeks they had invited and cajoled various members of the two congregations to undertake the preparation of savoury or sweet dishes. These were all to be delivered to the St Mary's church hall at least an hour before 'kickoff' so that they could be arranged as a buffet.

The buffet was to be at one end of the hall. At the other end was the stage on which would appear the various talents later in the evening. In between the buffet and the stage were arranged about twenty tables, each one of which was, at that very moment, being laid for eight people by a band of volunteers which included Dawn and Trevor Copeland, Alan Watts, Joy Bartholomew and Lynda.

When Lynda saw me looking around admiringly she moved towards me. Oh no, I thought, she's either going to give me a job to do, or take me to task once again over the planned 'watch'.

'Hello, Michael,' she said briskly, 'can I have a word?'

'Of course,' I said, bracing myself for the attack.

Lynda looked one way and then the other before adding, 'Somewhere more private. If you don't mind.'

I thought, 'Oh, dear', but said only 'Outside? Let's go outside.'

In the car park various people were still unloading foil-covered trays from the backs of cars. Colin was helping the vicar manoeuvre a pram full of bottles towards the hall door.

'Let's go round here,' I said quietly, leading Lynda through the gateway and into the garden at the back of the church. I decided to be bold.

'I think I know what you're going to say,' I ventured.

'You do!' Lynda exclaimed. Her face betrayed surprise, and not fury as I had expected.

'Well, it's the watch, I suppose,' I continued, rather sheepishly.

We had reached a wooden bench and sat down next to each other. Lynda's head was bent forward, and her long hair hung down over the shoulders of her Laura Ashley dress, obscuring her face for a few moments. When she looked up she was smiling. Now I really *was* confused.

She must have seen my confusion, and responded by saying, 'I'm not going to tell you I'm in favour of it, you know.'

'I didn't think you *would* be,' I said, before subsiding into silence. Lynda pushed her hair back and cleared her throat.

'But things have changed a bit,' she said. 'Have you got time?'

'Yes, of course,' I replied, managing not to look at my watch. 'What do you mean, things have changed?'

'After you'd been to the house the other day, I talked to Gordon about it. Well, *he* started the talking actually.'

I nodded, remembering the burly figure of Lynda's husband.

'To cut a long story short,' she continued, 'Gordon offered to help. With the watch, that is. He offered to help with the watch.'

Lynda fell silent and leaned forward, her hair once more falling across her face.

'Why should he have done that?' I asked as gently as I could. There was a pause before Lynda replied.

'I'm not altogether sure,' she said without looking up. 'He said he liked the idea. The idea of the scouts being in the church. He liked the idea that they were doing what they were doing, even though they weren't church people, as such. And he liked you.'

'Me?'

'Yes, you,' said Lynda, suddenly looking up and glowering at me. I caught a glimpse of what might have been a small tear in the corner of her eye. She seemed to realize that she had snapped at me, and breathed deeply before continuing.

'You know Gordon never comes to church. He never *has* done. He has a deep mistrust of everything to do with the church. Especially clergy. He can't abide clergy.'

She hesitated as if inviting a comment from me, but I stayed quiet. Over the garden wall I could hear the muted shrieks of the two Marys but couldn't discern whether it was mirth or despair.

'When I was filled with the Holy Spirit,' continued Lynda, 'soon after we were married, I hoped that Gordon would be filled too. But no. He has always shown a loving respect for me and my views. And I've always been praying for him – especially this year. I don't know why. It just seems to have felt more important this year. To me, I mean. Anyway, I'm rambling a bit, aren't I? What I wanted to say was that he likes you. He told me he thinks he could talk to you because you're different. You're not a clergyman who's tied to the church. That's what he said. He said you were more of a freelancer. A free spirit. That was the expression he used – free spirit.'

Lynda stopped and sniffed before going on.

'You see, Gordon's a free spirit in his own way. He used to be in the navy, roaming the world. Now he works freelance as a photographer. And he said he thought he could talk to you because you don't live off the church. Those are his words not mine. I wouldn't say that Canon George was living off the church. But you can see what he meant. Gordon thinks because you've got a job in the real world, you're more his sort. Do you see what I mean?'

A breeze had started to rustle the leaves around us. It was also pulling at Lynda's hair, making her look like some kind of pre-Raphaelite heroine.

'I'm very flattered,' I said at last. 'And that's why Gordon has volunteered to help with the watch?'

Lynda snorted slightly, regaining her composure in that instant.

'I think the watch is an excuse,' she said. 'I think he sees it as a good reason for spending some time away from me talking to you about . . .'

The words seemed to dry up.

'About?' I prompted quietly.

'I don't know,' Lynda went on. 'I honestly don't know. But I think he also did it as a gesture.'

'A gesture? What kind of gesture?'

'He knows I've been longing for him to set foot inside St Mary's. As soon as he could see how opposed I was to the watch, then he also saw how he could come into the church on his own terms. In a way that no one could trace back to my influence. And, of course, once he'd got *that* in his mind, well, then all the pieces started to fall into place.'

'What sort of pieces?'

'Oh, like the fact that he used to be a scout in the very same group. And you'll never guess who was the scout leader then?'

'Not Jack!'

'It certainly was,' said Lynda, managing a smile once again. 'I think that man's been around for ever.'

I laughed, trying to build on this small sign of levity. The air was getting cooler by the minute, however, and I knew that soon we would have to end the conversation.

'How do *you* feel about it all?' I asked.

'Hah!' said Lynda forcefully. It was something of a dramatic and self-conscious expression, and I took encouragement from that.

'How do you expect me to feel? First of all, I was very cross about it. And then upset.'

'And now?'

Lynda looked me straight in the eye.

'Now I think that God may be using this to tell me

130

something. And perhaps even to call Gordon to him.'

My face was expressionless as I stared into Lynda's now blissfully calm eyes. Of all the people in the congregation, Lynda was probably the only one who could look me in the eye and speak with such conviction about what God was doing. In the end, I had to look away, conscious of the many questions that continually buzzed in my head on occasions such as this.

But this was not a time for those questions. I looked back and Lynda's face was unchanged, a picture of serene acceptance after the turbulence of the preceding minutes.

'I've prayed so much for him, and last night I felt that the Holy Spirit was moving in his life as in mine. Do you see?'

I sighed. It may have looked like agreement, but was more a sign of bewilderment.

'Does this mean that you're happy for the watch to go ahead?' I said, feeling that I now had to move the conversation through to some kind of practical conclusion.

Lynda smiled again.

'I told you just now,' she said. 'I'm not going to say I'm in favour of it. As I said, things have changed. I want Gordon to be in the church. I want him to talk to you. I want your two free spirits to come together in some way. And, of course, I want the Holy Spirit to be the reason and purpose of that coming together. If that has to be on the Eve of All Hallows of all nights, then so be it. God moves in mysterious ways.'

'You can say that again!' I said, rising to my feet. 'Come on, let's get back to the hall before we start any rumours. Otherwise your husband might feel he wants to talk to me about something less spiritual!'

Lynda's laugh seemed to seal our conversation with

the friendship which I had always felt underpinned our differences.

As we neared the church hall once again, the buzz of activity became ever more noticeable. Lynda walked away from me without another word and disappeared into a group of people chattering by the door.

* * *

Cheryl arrived soon afterwards, having left Amy in the capable care of Martha Cummings from number twenty-four. My wife and I found ourselves on a table with the Copelands (who had also left young children with baby-sitters) and two couples from St John's whom neither of us knew very well.

We all ate substantial meals of quiche, salad, baked potatoes, and more quiche.

'I do like a bit of quiche,' said Trevor Copeland new-manfully and very diplomatically.

'Oh, do you?' shrieked a passing Mary. 'Well, here, have some more.'

Trevor managed a smile as another large slice was deposited on his plate. His attempts to share it with the rest of us at the table were unsuccessful.

'Couldn't eat another thing.'

'It does look good, but I'm rather full myself.'

'No. You go ahead. Don't worry about us.'

Dessert was a choice of rhubarb crumble and custard or lemon cheesecake. Cheryl and I both opted for the crumble, having been told earlier by Colin that Doreen's rhubarb was beyond comparison. We then helped ourselves to coffee from a large urn, and made ourselves comfortable for the 'Hidden Talents'.

My decision not to appear was easily made. I have no *obvious* talent, let alone any that is hidden. For Cheryl the matter was less clear-cut. Cheryl had been a dancer in the years before Amy's birth, and would have been more than capable of entertaining the assembled company in some way. Her decision not to appear was mainly due to lack of time.

'If I'm to arrange some kind of dance,' she had said, implying that this would be an organized team effort, 'then I need more time than I currently have with the job and looking after your daughter!'

I wasn't going to risk any verbal abuse by suggesting otherwise. Anyway, I reflected, my role as unpaid curate probably meant that the Dunn family already had more than its fair share of church-based amateur dramatics.

The lights dimmed, and Colin switched on the two spotlights that stood on stands at either side of the hall. Suddenly there was a burst of ragged applause as Canon George appeared through the gap in the curtains.

'Good evening, everyone,' he boomed. 'Well, that was a good welcome, especially considering I've done nothing! I hope you'll be even more appreciative of the people who have cast modesty to the winds this evening and who will, in a few moments' time, reveal their hidden talents. But before we begin I would like to make one announcement. I'll be as brief as possible. The work on St Mary's has finished. The church will reopen at the end of next week.'

His words were drowned in another burst of applause that this time was loud and long. For many people those words confirmed what they had already heard on the grapevine. For others, the same words were unexpected. For all concerned they were the cause of joyous celebration.

Canon George smiled beatifically at everyone and tried to restore order by raising his hands.

'More of that anon,' he said. 'But, for now, on with

the motley, as they say. The show must go on. And what a show we have for you tonight. There are five talents in all and so, without further ado, let the revelation begin!'

There was a hush of anticipation through the hall as the curtains were pulled back to reveal four adolescent members of the St Mary's choir dressed in lederhosen. One of them strummed a chord on the guitar, and then the other three chimed in with a rendition of 'Edelweiss'. The woman sitting next to me leaned over and whispered in my ear the single word 'Charming!'

'Indeed,' I whispered back.

The song came to an end and was met by rapturous applause. The four adolescents looked somewhat bemused by this and, after a few moments of intense conferring, signalled that they would do an encore. The applause died down, and we all settled back in our seats in anticipation of another song.

Once again, the youth with the guitar strummed a chord, and then the group began to sing 'Edelweiss' once again. The woman sitting next to me leaned across again and whispered, 'I think they only know this one.'

It was noticeable that, when the song ended, the applause was somewhat more restrained. Clearly, people were afraid that to show too much enthusiasm would be to tempt a third rendition of the by now familiar little number.

Indeed, it seemed as if a salutary lesson had been learned by all concerned. From that moment on most of the evening's applause was kept at a respectful level without becoming over-enthusiastic.

Next was Christine, a short, wide woman with short, wide hair, dressed in a bright magenta T-shirt and lime green leggings. Christine began to throw a blue ball up into the air and then catch it. To this she added a yellow ball, and then an orange ball.

The woman next to me once more gave me the benefit of her prescience.

'She's juggling,' she said.

'I think you may be right,' I replied, beginning to become just a fraction irritated by her commentary. I turned back to watch Christine give a very competent display of juggling, before ending with a short speech on the therapeutic merits of the exercise. She explained how it was perfect for relieving stress and how it was something that could be undertaken with very little equipment or training.

'Balls,' said the woman next to me. I turned around and stared at her. 'You need balls,' she added. 'Or Indian clubs, or whatever it is they call those things.'

'Right,' I said, turning back towards the stage, where Canon George was announcing the next talent.

'You all know Geoffrey Newton,' said the vicar. 'Well, many of you will not know that Geoffrey is something of an impressionist. So, tonight, listen out for a few familiar voices in a sketch which he has called "Today in Parliament".'

Geoffrey began. I didn't immediately recognize the voice he was 'doing', but then I have to admit that I am no expert on matters parliamentary. I glanced across at Cheryl for a clue, but Cheryl was also looking mystified.

'Who's he supposed to be?' mouthed Cheryl.

'I've no idea,' I mouthed back.

Fortunately, the woman next to me was able to fill us in.

'He's that one . . . you know . . . that Mr . . . er . . . the one who . . .,' she began, before confirming 'He's that politician. You know. The one on the telly.'

Cheryl and I both expressed our thanks to the woman for illuminating our darkness. In the meantime, Geoffrey had switched voices and put on a pair of spectacles. Cheryl and I again looked at each other blankly.

At this point, Trevor Copeland, who is not normally one to make derisory comments, said in a loud stage whisper, 'Which Parliament *is* this exactly? The Parliament of Uzbekistan?'

I managed to stifle a giggle, but lost control when the woman next to me said, 'Oh, no. I think he would have said. I'm sure it's *our* Parliament he's doing.'

I pretended to have something stuck in my throat and reached for a glass of water. Fortunately, Geoffrey's talent did not quite stretch to an attempt at the *whole* Cabinet, and he soon left the stage to muted but sympathetic applause.

'Today in Parliament' was soon forgotten as John and Rose Burgess swept into view dressed as two ancient Egyptians, accompanied by Malcolm on the piano. I didn't have to look at Cheryl to know that she was biting her lip and fighting to maintain some semblance of calm.

John and Rose Burgess – 'the Prophets' as Stephen and I called them – were two of the most fearsome-looking individuals one could hope to meet. Their constant mission seemed always to point out the errors of the church and all those involved in it. The mere thought of their Egyptian dance had, when I first heard of it, set up a curious wave of anticipation in my very soul. To see them now, in the flesh, snaking their way backwards and forwards across the stage in long black wigs and looking like a suburban version of Akhenaton and Nefertiti, was a sight without parallel.

It was another one of those occasions when hysteria seemed just around the corner. Just so long as no one says anything to me, I thought, I'll be all right. It was just at that moment that the woman sitting next to me poked me in the back. When I turned round she held a folded piece of paper in front of my face.

'A note for you,' she said. 'From Father Stephen. On the next table.'

I looked across to the next table, but Stephen was staring seriously at the stage. I then opened the piece of paper on which were written the following words:

A message to the Prophets:
Matthew 2:13 – 'Flee to Egypt and remain there till I tell you.'

That was it. That did it. I shrieked, spluttered, and quickly – learning from past experience – stuffed a handkerchief in my mouth. Cheryl looked away and tried to pretend that she didn't know me. I attempted to take my mind off the absurdity of the situation by reciting in my head all the books of the Old Testament. Unfortunately, however, Exodus immediately set me off again into another fit of giggles.

It took some time for the storm to calm, and I was only able to replace the handkerchief in my pocket just as John and Rose Burgess were taking their final bow.

'And now for our finale,' boomed Canon George, as the applause faded away. 'It's time for the parish's Vera Lynn to lead us all in a singsong. So please put your hands together for your very own Barbara Bailey!'

This was the sign for everyone in the hall over the age of seventy to go mildly ecstatic. Indeed, there was even a bit of foot-stamping as Barbara Bailey, looking for all the world like a member of the Royal Family, took to the stage to lead the singing of 'We'll meet again'.

Barbara had given up her place in the choir some years before when she took on the duties of sacristan at St Mary's, although her voice was always very evident at church. It was a powerful and largely tuneful voice, but nevertheless one of those tremulous voices that makes every note seem as if it might develop into something resembling an Alpine yodel.

One thing, however, was without doubt. Barbara Bailey commanded absolute respect from the combined congregations of St Mary's and St John's. During the bits which she sang alone, not even the woman next to me dared whisper a word. And when Barbara signalled that it was time to join in with a chorus, everyone did his or her best to make some kind of vocal contribution (albeit, as in my case, an inconspicuous hum).

It was a remarkable display of a particular kind of celebration. A celebration that looked back perhaps more than it looked forward. There was, after all, a lot of nostalgia about it. But why not? For Barbara, for Doreen, for Frank, Colin and all the older stalwarts of the parish, the church building that had been part of their lives for so long was about to be part of their lives again. A kind of victory had been won.

For me, as always, the situation seemed more ambiguous. For me this was not so much the end of a restoration, but rather (I hoped) the start of a renewal. In two weeks' time I would be ordained as a priest. Many things, not least the conversation with Lynda earlier in the evening, had convinced me that my mission lay less in buildings and more in people. Less in keeping alive an established church, and more in making the church a place where people could find spiritual freedom.

On the way home I shrugged off such philosophical

thoughts and laughed about the evening's show. I suggested to Cheryl that some of those particular talents would have been better off staying buried.

'That's not only unkind,' said Cheryl. 'It's unfair and it's also untrue. You once said you wanted to set people free. Well, if you're serious about that, you ought to show a bit more respect when they reveal the bits of themselves they normally keep hidden.'

I looked suitably mortified and mumbled an apology. But, even as I did so, my mind filled with the memory of the Prophets and Stephen's note. Two hours later, in bed, I was still trying to control the giggles, and Cheryl pretended to be cross, which only made things worse.

NINE

Open for Business

> Like living stones, let yourselves be built into a
> spiritual house to be a holy priesthood.
> 1 Peter 2:5

It was a Wednesday at the very end of September, and the last vestiges of a short Indian summer were fading into the mists of autumn. There was an air of mellowness hanging like a milky haze over the whole of creation.

Well, perhaps not the *whole* of creation.

'Yes, I know you've had it booked for months,' said Philip. 'And, yes, I know you can't get out of it. But that doesn't make it any easier for the rest of us. The fact remains that Crombies chose the agency largely because of you. And now, just as we come to our first crunch meeting with them, you're not going to be around.'

I kept quiet. I wasn't sure if I was angry or whether I simply felt sorry for Philip.

'I mean,' he continued, when it was clear that I was not about to volunteer any compromise on this issue. 'The service – your ordination, or whatever the term is – is on Sunday, isn't it? Why can't you go wherever it is you have to go tomorrow, come back here for the meeting on Friday, and then go back to your . . . your treat . . . whatever you call it?'

'*Re*treat,' I said flatly. 'It's called a retreat. Not a treat.'

'Retreat then,' said Philip, who was beginning to be irritated by my obvious unwillingness to meet him (as he would have put it) 'halfway'. 'Why can't you go there *after* the meeting?'

I breathed slowly. The diocese, I knew, had strong views about the need for ordinands to be on retreat for the whole of the designated period – that is, from midday on Thursday until Sunday morning and the trip to the cathedral. I also knew, however, that if I were sufficiently assertive, or preferably just canny, I would be able to slip away from the retreat for a few hours on the Friday without upsetting too many people.

But that was not the point. The point was that I had to draw, metaphorically speaking, a line in the sand.

For a number of years I had very consciously decided to follow through a calling to the ministry within the context of my secular job. Increasingly my thoughts about how that should work in practice were becoming clearer. I knew, for example, that I wanted to move away from seeing my working life in terms of two areas of employment. I wanted to move towards a situation where there was just one area – a genuine combination of secular work and ministry. More than that, I had decided some months before that such a situation could only work if I gave my advertising job as much respect as I did my 'ministry'. If *I* did not fully respect what I was doing, then I could hardly expect others to do so. And if others respected what I was doing in terms of my secular activity, they might then also begin to see 'where I was coming from' in terms of the more spiritual dimension.

Well, that was the theory, at least.

The problem was that the ordination was different. This was, after all, the event that would provide the public confirmation and affirmation of what I had felt to be a calling as a priest. This would, I trusted, be one of the foundation stones on which my ministry could be built. Something on which I would be able to draw for strength and inspiration when things got rough.

It was twelve months before that I had been ordained for the first time as a deacon. It was now time for me to be ordained a second time, as a priest – ordained into a role that would give me wider scope for carrying through God's work in the parish, even if, ultimately, it made no great practical difference to the way I conducted myself as a Christian at work.

At this special time, probably more than at any other time in my life, I owed it to God, and to everyone with whom I would live and work in the months and years to come, to devote myself to prayer and reflection for the three days before Sunday. *That* was the point.

I simply could not say yes to Philip's request. It would be a dereliction of duty far greater, in my estimation, than missing a meeting with an important client. It was, I felt, a wholly honourable position to have taken. And yet it was also a position that might appear unworldly and somewhat precious.

It was then that a thought struck me. It was, in some ways, a rather underhand thought. But, then again, it was probably also true.

'Philip,' I said, ending a lengthy silence just as he was beginning to turn bright pink with frustration. He looked at me hopefully. 'Philip, what do you think the people at Crombies would say if they knew that I had given their meeting priority over something very important – a matter of conscience and duty – that had been in everyone's diary for more than six months? Do you think they would trust me to deal with their business in a straight and honest way if they felt my sense of loyalty was just a tiny bit . . . elastic?'

Philip's impetuous nature already had him opening

his mouth to speak the words of pragmatic rebuttal. But he stopped in mid-gape, turned away from me and stared hard at a picture on the wall of his office.

'You *may* be right,' he said at last, still looking away from me. 'I could say that you felt they would understand. That you were already committed somewhere else. I could tell them exactly what it was. I could tell them that in the future *they* could expect the same level of commitment from you. From *us*, I mean. What do you think?'

He turned round, his high brow furrowed in thought.

'I think you have to say what you feel to be right,' I replied, slightly pompously, before adding, 'You could just tell them the truth.'

'Of course,' said Philip quickly, as if the thought of saying anything else were totally abhorrent. I managed to keep the smile off my face. 'The truth, hmm, yes,' he ruminated. 'The truth. *That* should do it.'

He smiled for the first time during our session together, clearly pleased that he had hit upon this clever wheeze.

'OK,' he said, rather dismissively. 'Good. Well, you have a good . . . whatever it is. And I'll see you on Monday. Don't worry about Crombies. I'll look after that.'

I rose from the low leather chair and smiled back at Philip. As I left his office I said I would try not to worry about Crombies.

When I arrived home that evening Amy helped me to pack for the retreat.

'I've put Dolly in your bag in case you get lonely without me and Mummy. Don't lose her!'

I thanked her and insisted that, although I thought she was the best cook in the world – after Mummy, of course – I really, *really* would prefer not to have one of her cakes rolled up in my brand-new clerical shirt. This particular shirt was very dark blue, with small gold alphas and omegas all over it.

Amy said she could see that it was perhaps not the best place for the cake, and so stuffed it inside my shoe instead. As it was Amy's bedtime, and with a view to curtailing her provision of 'help', I whisked her off to her room and read her the beginning of *Matilda* before returning to where Cheryl was still sitting on the side of the bed next to my suitcase.

'Would you have put the retreat ahead of me and Amy?' she asked archly after I had told her about my conversation with Philip and how I thought he had taken a very narrow view of things. 'What would you have done if *I* had asked you to be here on Friday? If I'd been tied up at work and the child-minder was ill, and Amy was unhappy. Would you have come away *then*?'

I carried on packing whilst I thought about my answer.

'That's a bit unfair,' I said after a few moments. 'You wouldn't *ask* me to be here. You'd get out of your lecture or your meeting or whatever it was. Wouldn't you?'

'Well, we've never discussed it actually,' said Cheryl. 'It's rather been taken for granted that the retreat would come first, hasn't it? Oh, don't look so hurt. I'm not moaning. I'm just stating it as a matter of fact. We have, both of us, just assumed that the retreat came first. We've done that because its build-up has played such a big part in our lives. For other people, that's not the case. As far as Philip is concerned, he's always just assumed that work comes first. He probably always will. Don't get me wrong. I'm not defending him. But in a way his view is no more narrow than yours. It's just different, that's all.'

I stood still for a second, a pair of socks in one hand and a pair of briefs in the other.

'Possibly,' I said grudgingly. 'Now, where's my travelling alarm clock?'

* * *

Following the rather frenetic pilgrimage to the cathedral in a series of cars twelve months before, the diocese had decided that this year they did not want to risk the uncertainty as to whether everyone – or, indeed, anyone – would turn up on time. So it was that the deacons who were to be ordained priests were asked to meet at the cathedral on the Thursday for a rehearsal, after which we would all be taken by coach to the retreat house. This coach would then bring us back to the mother church for the Sunday morning.

As I walked into Southwark Cathedral, the first thing I saw was the large body of Rita, the Croydon sculptress. Rita's bulky frame was draped in a voluminous and exotic dress. I was soon to have a very close-up view of the pattern of the dress, as Rita swept towards me and clasped me to her ample bosom in something of a bear-hug.

'You're not well,' she said, releasing me at last.

'Yes, I am,' I insisted weakly.

'No, you're not,' she asserted. 'I can tell. You've been working too hard.'

There was no point in arguing. Rita always knew better than anyone else.

'And how are *you*, Rita?'

Rita leaned forward conspiratorially.

'I'm in transition, darling. Painful, but necessary. I'll tell you more another time.'

Just as well, I thought, as I was quite unsure

whether this statement was a reference to work, the church, accommodation, relationships, or anything else for that matter.

Past Rita's substantial shoulder I could see several other fellow deacons moving towards us.

'Ken!' I boomed. 'How good to see you!'

Ken proffered a damp and limp hand which I squeezed affectionately before returning it to his safe keeping.

Rosemary, looking cuddly and motherly as always, held both my hands and gave me a big kiss before leading me over to where the stout and bearded Brian was talking to Dr Soley, the principal of SLOP, the South London Ordination Programme.

Brian crushed my hand in his as a sign of brotherly love, whilst Dr Soley placed his skeletal fingers on my shoulder. Whilst I am sure this was meant as a sign of forgiveness and possibly affection, it nevertheless gave me the impression that I had been apprehended in some way by the ecclesiastical establishment, and was being taken in hand.

'And how is your ministry going, Michael?' asked Dr Soley.

'Like a bat out of hell!' I said enthusiastically.

Now, quite *why* I said this, I am at a loss to know. For some perverse reason, those were the first words that sprang to my lips, and I spent the next minute or so in grovelling mode, trying to regain some semblance of sympathy from my erstwhile principal.

I then attempted to convey in a few further sentences something of the practical and emotional turmoil that seemed to have characterized my first twelve months in holy orders. As I continued to rattle on in this rather frantic and apologetic vein, I could see the smile gradually draining from Dr Soley's face. By

146

the end of my discursive narrative, he appeared quite world-weary.

'Well, it sounds as if you've had some interesting experiences', he said tiredly, before slipping away to talk to someone – anyone – who had had rather fewer interesting experiences.

The rehearsal began and proceeded uneventfully. Uneventful, that is, in terms of what appeared on the surface. Beneath the serious expressions and immaculate robes, our combined emotions were clearly in a highly excited state. The ordination for which we were preparing would be the first priesting in the cathedral of both men and women. The first ordination of women to the priesthood had taken place only a few months before, and hopes and fears from all quarters were only too apparent.

Perhaps because of that the rehearsal was taut with unexpressed joy and unreleased anxiety. The air was pregnant with emotions that could only be born three days hence. It was as if there needed to be some acknowledgement of a death before there could be a wholehearted embracing of the resurrection. And as if all our personal journeys were, at the very same moment, both the biggest things and the smallest things imaginable.

That feeling stayed with us even when we disrobed, and the drive to the retreat house was a muted affair, as most people sat quietly, beginning to come to terms with the reality of the situation. I opened my Bible and read from the First Letter of Peter, 'Like living stones, let yourselves be built into a spiritual house to be a holy priesthood'. They were words which set off a whole cascade of thoughts in my head. About my own church and the small stones that had fallen on my head. About its people, the *real* foundations of its life. About the church's potential as a spiritual house. About all these things built together as a holy priesthood, in which my own role, as a publicly affirmed priest, would be just one small representative part.

It was all too much to take in. I closed my Bible and gazed distractedly at a kaleidoscopic South London spinning past my window.

* * *

Our time at the retreat house, from Thursday afternoon to Saturday evening, was not all given over to muted reflection. There were plenty of quiet times, but also several noisy times as well. As much laughter as there were tears. By early Sunday morning, everyone seemed to have found some kind of equilibrium between the two, and we began to look forward to the day ahead with unabashed excitement. Breakfast was a calm and even jolly affair, and we loaded ourselves into the coach with the sort of knock-about enthusiasm that used to characterize the best school outings when I was a child.

'Wonderful shirt,' purred Rita, pawing at me with her plump, ringed fingers. 'It makes you look like a god.'

She laughed raucously as Ken, clearly disapproving of her comments and familiarity, slid into the seat in front of us next to Rosemary.

'Ken,' I called. 'Show us *your* shirt. It's new, isn't it?'

Ken stood up rather sheepishly, and slipped off his jacket to reveal a new black clerical shirt that I thought looked very Rome-ish with its narrow opening at the neck.

'My Aunt Margaret bought it for me,' Ken said proudly. 'She sent it in the post last week. Trouble is, it's a wee bit too big.'

So saying he demonstrated the point by pushing the whole of his fist into the gap between his neck and the collar.

'Never mind,' said Rita. 'You'll grow into it.'

Ken looked as if he wasn't too happy about the prospect of having his neck expand sufficiently to fill the shirt.

'It's very Catholic,' I said provocatively. 'You know, very Rome-ish. Makes you look like a Catholic priest. Don't you agree, Father Brian? Don't you think Father Kenneth here could be on his way to Rome?'

Brian laughed. Ken looked mortified.

'I . . . I . . . I . . .' he stammered, 'I'm only wearing it for Aunt Margaret. I thought it would please her. Do you really think it makes me look like a Roman Catholic?'

Brian, Rita and I nodded gravely.

'It could be all up for you in the parish,' I said with mock seriousness, 'when your flock see that you've "gone over".'

Brian was giggling uncontrollably. Rosemary popped her head up to look at me with one of her 'Oh, you shouldn't tease him so much, you know' faces. Ken was already hunting through his holdall in search of his other clerical shirt, and muttering things like 'It's in here somewhere, I know it is. My old pale blue one.'

I settled back into my seat to enjoy the journey, whilst in front of me Ken was stripping off the offending shirt. Whatever else this day would mean to each of us in our hearts, the whole event was clearly also something of a public performance. A public performance in a world where the shape, size and colour of shirts still mattered.

Other than Ken's striptease, the journey was less dramatic than our trip the year before. We arrived at the cathedral with plenty of time before the service, and I was grateful for the opportunity to soak up the atmosphere. Whereas the last occasion had overawed me, I was acutely aware that *this* time was my second, and therefore my last, ordination. I not only wanted to enjoy the day, I wanted to remember as much of it as possible. I wanted to be aware of the details. I wanted to let the sights, the sounds and even the smells all make their appropriate impressions so that, in years to come, I might be able to bring it all to mind.

With these thoughts in my head, I stood in my cassock at the back of the cathedral. There was still forty minutes to go before the service was due to start when a woman I did not know approached me.

'Michael Dunn?' she asked tentatively.

I turned to look at a pretty face framed by long curly brown hair.

'I just wanted to wish you good luck,' she continued. 'If that's what you wish people at times like this. I don't know really.' She laughed an embarrassed laugh. 'Oh, yes,' she added, 'and to say "thank you". I don't know what you said to him that time, but it seems to have made a difference. And he always talks about it. About you, I mean. Thanks.'

I found my voice at last.

'I'm sorry,' I said. 'But . . .'

'You don't know who I am, do you? I'm Anne. Thanks again.'

And with that, she rushed away, disappearing quickly into the growing crowd of people who were filing into the building.

I only saw her again as we processed into the space of the cathedral to the strains of 'I was glad'. There she was, standing against the wall at the back of the building, close to where she had spoken to me. And there standing next to her was Chris Mulligan, grinning at me like a Cheshire cat.

It was such an unexpected moment in what I had imagined would be a familiar perambulation, that I immediately felt a large lump in my throat and walked the rest of the way along the central aisle with tears filling my eyes. As I sat in my place a few feet from the bishop's throne, I peered around, trying to see Cheryl and Amy. There they were, sitting near the front, almost out of my range of vision. They had arrived quite late and we hadn't had a chance to speak before the service. Cheryl returned my look with a serene smile and Amy gave me a wave.

From then on, and despite my clear intentions, I remember very little. Except that when it came to the Sharing of the Peace I was able to find Cheryl and Amy in the sea of bodies that had filled the aisle like the waters of the Red Sea crashing down after the Israelites had crossed to safety. When I hugged them it was as if I had never really hugged them before, and my tears mingled with theirs in the midst of a flood of faces.

'You're a priest,' blubbed Cheryl.

'I know,' I blubbed back.

'What's it like, Daddy?' called Amy, pulling on my stole.

'I don't know,' I said truthfully. 'I really don't know.'

We hugged each other again.

'Do you want to know something else?' said Cheryl.

I looked back at her blankly as if somehow this were all happening to someone else.

'I'm pregnant,' she said. 'I found out on Friday.'

That did it. If we were a hopeless mess of emotions *before* that moment, we were an even greater one after it.

'I'll see you later,' I said weakly, turning to retake my place at the front of the cathedral.

'I do hope so!' said Cheryl with a smile. 'We've a long way to go yet.'

* * *

Days are funny things. What was it Philip Larkin said? 'Days are where we live.' Some slip by in a coat of anonymity; we hardly know they have been and gone. Some measure out each waking hour as if hanging on grimly to a ration of time. Others are no more than a flash caught fleetingly like a yellow splash of light on chrome. This one was bursting with richness, almost *too* rich, like swollen fruit.

Drained by the ordination, exhilarated by Cheryl's news, this was not a day on which to drive. I was very grateful, therefore, to find that Penny Wainwright had brought my family to the cathedral, and was happy to take us all back. Back to a few more hugs, two glasses of champagne, a light lunch, and then three hours of dreamless sleep.

When I awoke late in the afternoon it was to climb once more on to the whirligig of this quite extraordinary day. For more was to come. At half past seven in the evening I was to preside at my first Eucharist at St Mary's.

Did I say my words correctly? Did I perform according to plan? Did I come up to scratch? I honestly couldn't say. You would have to ask someone else. All I know is that the whole event felt like a thanksgiving. For St Mary's. For the congregation, who had worked so hard to have the place open once more. And, in the case of the Dunn family, for the news that (God willing) our family would be increased in the months to follow.

The service began with some words of blessing for a beautiful oak stool that stood proudly to one side of the sanctuary. It finished with my standing at the door to receive the congratulations of the many folk who were there as they made their way out of the building and over to the church hall for drinks.

'Well done, *Father*,' said Doreen, with an unusual and pronounced emphasis on the word.

'Thank you, Doreen,' I said. 'News travels fast, doesn't it?'

Doreen looked at me with that tolerant but stony gaze that she reserved for drunks, lunatics and curates, before smiling sympathetically at Cheryl, who was standing at my side.

'She was making a point of calling you "Father" because it's your first Eucharist, you blockhead,' said Cheryl, as Doreen moved away. 'Not because I'm pregnant. No one knows *that* yet.'

'Oh,' I said, somewhat lamely, before turning to face the queue of people who wished to shake my hand.

Once in the hall I found myself surrounded by all the figures who, in their own very different ways, had been important influences on my first year as a clergyman. Colin, complete as ever in his cassock and making small jerky movements of an unnecessarily subservient kind in the direction of the new priest. Geoffrey Newton, slapping me on the back, and asking very irreverently whether I was now entitled to join the magic circle. Alan Watts, within minutes of my arriving, presenting me with a rota containing the dates of all my proposed weekly Eucharists up to Christmas. Christine asking me about Hildegard of Bingen, and looking disappointed when I replied that surely Bingen was a football club in the Danish first division, and Hildegard its top scorer.

John Burgess, overhearing my flippancy, hove into view with the following words: 'Leviticus 4:3. "If it is the anointed priest who sins, thus bringing guilt on the people, then let him offer for the sin which he has committed a young bull without blemish to the Lord for a sin offering".'

I looked at John, and then at Christine, and then at John once more. Both were staring back at me and I was totally unsure as to who was kidding whom.

'Well, thank you for sharing that with us, John,' I said at last. 'Perhaps if you should hear of any young bulls without blemish, you could let me know.'

With those words, I swiftly moved on, only to find myself encompassed by a brace of Marys. Each Mary grabbed one of my elbows and, amid much smiling and chortling, steered me over to a table on which were several bowls of nibbles.

'Canapés,' said Mary West triumphantly. 'And with asparagus. Mary made them specially for you.'

I turned to Mary Brown who was fluttering her eyelashes for all she was worth. I bent over and gave her a big kiss whilst she continued to mutter things like 'No, really', 'No, you mustn't', and 'It was nothing'.

It was at this point that Joy Bartholomew arrived on the scene.

'Do you know?' she said, chuckling quietly to herself. 'That was always my father's favourite.'

'Asparagus?' I said, feeling that this was a safe, if unadventurous, response.

'No,' said Joy, looking bemused at my clear lack of insight as to her father's taste. 'Gooseberries.'

Fortunately Frank was on hand to lead me away.

'Come on,' he said, only too aware that he was saving me from a potential string of *non sequiturs*,

'Come and say hello to a friend of ours.'

He guided me tactfully but firmly past a number of faces who seemed anxious to engage me in conversation. They included the formidable figures of Lynda, Hilary and Barbara. But Frank was not to be deterred. With his arm through mine, he led me out of the lion's den and into a quiet corner where I found myself face-to-face with the tanned expression and grizzled hair that I now knew well.

'I'll leave you two to have a natter,' said Frank, disappearing once more into the throng.

'Peter,' I said simply, holding out my hand. 'I'm so glad you came. It's really good to see you.'

Peter Strang held my hand in his and gave it a reassuring squeeze.

'Big day,' he said gruffly. 'Lot of people.' He looked past my shoulder at the mêlée beyond. It was clearly not a situation in which he felt particularly comfortable, and I was immediately aware of how much he was giving me simply by being there.

'The stool is beautiful,' I said at once, keen to anchor the conversation in what we had in common.

He nodded, the wrinkles of his face creasing into a smile.

'Did it serve?' he asked, somewhat gravely. 'Its purpose, I mean. What it was made for.'

I smiled back.

'It served,' I said, conscious of the rather odd word, and wanting to play it back to the master carpenter. 'And will continue to serve,' I added. 'I'm sure of it.'

The crowd in the hall had expanded to the point where it was about to enclose Peter and I within its murmuring embrace. In the instant that I felt Canon George at my elbow, to fetch me for an official presentation, I saw Peter tip his head in a movement of

155

parting. The next moment, Peter had disappeared, and I was being led, once more, back through the people to take up a position at the front.

* * *

Dawn Copeland had taken Amy home with her children immediately after the service, leaving Cheryl and me to play out our roles as the clergy couple.

By the time we arrived home it was nearly midnight. I was conscious that I had to be at work the next morning, but could still not resist the temptation to pour Cheryl and myself one more celebratory drink. As I was uncorking a bottle of wine, Cheryl called from the study.

'There's a fax here for you. Looks like it came a couple of hours ago. It's from Philip.'

'Oh, no!' I breathed, collapsing on to the sofa in the drawing room. 'What does it say?'

I looked up. Cheryl was standing in the doorway holding the piece of paper in her hands and smiling broadly. 'It says "Congratulations and well done!"'

I gulped, spluttered and sat up. 'It does?' I said incredulously. 'Congratulations?'

'Oh, yes,' said Cheryl. 'And there's a PS.'

I looked at her warily.

'It says "Michael, can we build on this? How about pitching for some church business?"'

Cheryl fell on to the sofa next to me, spilling my drink. And we laughed, and laughed, and laughed.

TEN

Midnight Sun

Now before faith came, we were imprisoned.
Galatians 3:23

It was with some trepidation that I packed my things on the afternoon of Halloween. It was a Saturday, and Amy sat cross-legged on the bed watching intently as I rolled up my sleeping bag.

'Are there any beds in the church?' she asked.

'I'm afraid not,' I said. 'I wish there were.'

'So where will you sleep, Daddy?'

'On the floor, I expect,' I said without any enthusiasm. 'There's some carpet in the sanctuary. I'll be all right on that.'

'What's that?' persisted Amy. 'What's that *sank* thing?'

'The sanctuary?' I replied. 'It's the bit at the front of the church. Where the big table is. Where I stand when I'm doing the . . .' I stopped myself from saying 'the magic'. '. . .when I'm doing the service.'

'Oh,' said Amy, by now clearly bored by the apparently pointless nature of this expedition. She slipped off the bed without another word and went to see if Mummy was doing something more interesting.

The three of us had an early supper together, and then later I set off in the car for St Mary's where I would meet the others who were to be part of the watch.

When I arrived at the church porch, the other three 'minders' were already there. Jack and Don, I knew,

157

would only be part of the group until midnight. Eight of the scouts had volunteered to be involved in the watch – the others preferring to save their strength for a sponsored sailing programme the following day.

When Gordon Soames had offered to help, I suggested to Jack that he and Don might wish to give the watch a miss in favour of the activities on the river. In the end we agreed on something of a compromise. The two scout leaders would spend some time with the watchers, whilst also guaranteeing themselves a good night's sleep prior to the Sunday sailing. It was an arrangement that had been agreed to by all the parents.

After saying hello to Jack and Don, I made a point of offering a special greeting to the burly figure of Gordon, Lynda's husband.

'It really is very good of you to volunteer for this,' I said, shaking his hand as warmly as I could.

'Think nothing of it,' said Gordon. 'I'm looking forward to this. It takes me back to the days when I used to be one of this old buffer's scouts.'

Gordon clapped Jack affectionately on the shoulder, before adding, 'Mind you, if I'd known there was sailing on tomorrow, I might have gone for that instead.'

'Did you know Gordon used to be in the Royal Navy?' said Jack.

'I think so,' I replied.

'Well, in the few minutes before you arrived,' continued Jack, 'we've lined him up to be the judge for our photography competition – and now we're working on him to become a full-time leader.'

Jack laughed, Gordon smiled and said, 'Whoa! Steady on!', and Don grunted his approval of the proceedings.

'I think we'd better see how tonight works out first of all,' said Gordon. 'I might not be the man for the job. Talking of which – when do the kids arrive?'

'In about half an hour,' I said. 'After *we've* had a chance to get ourselves a bit organized. And you'd better not call them kids. Well, not to their faces anyway!'

Gordon nodded knowingly, and swung a kitbag over his shoulder as I unlocked the door to let us in.

'There's quite a breeze getting up,' he said as we moved from the small porch into the apparent vastness of the church. 'I hope the kids – I mean the scouts – will be warm enough.'

'Oh, I've no doubt of that,' said Jack. 'They've each been told to bring two sleeping bags, a blanket or quilt, and two extra jumpers. They'll probably have more equipment than Scott of the Antarctic.'

We laughed, and then stood in silence, taking in the size and beauty of the church. I realized then that Jack and Don had probably not seen it empty and unlit before. Gordon had perhaps not been inside St Mary's for a very long time.

'A cold place.'

The three words fell like pieces of lead into the pool of shadowy stillness. Jack, Gordon and I looked round towards Don who had made one of his rare utterances.

'The church?' I asked.

'The Antarctic,' said Don flatly. 'It's a cold place.'

'You can say that again,' said Gordon, who seemed not at all surprised by Don's train of thought.

Jack and I nodded profoundly. I then went to turn on the lights and Jack began to unpack the various provisions that he had brought with him.

Within twenty minutes the scouts had started to arrive. First through the door were the Browning brothers, Adam and Edwin. Then came Gemma, and then five other scouts, all of whom I knew, at least by sight.

'Why are the lights on?' said Edwin somewhat indignantly.

'So that we can see what we're doing,' I replied.

'But you can't see a ghost when it's light,' he said with unswerving certainty. 'You can only see a ghost if it's dark.'

I decided not to argue with this logic, but instead said only, 'We'll turn most of the lights off when it's time to go to sleep.'

'Sleep?' cried Edwin incredulously. 'I'm not sleeping. Not me. Not all night. I'm staying awake. To see *him*.'

This last word was emphasized with a threatening intonation. So much for my attempts to position this event as something rather more – and less – than a 'ghost watch'.

Once the scouts had piled their several bags and blankets on top of ours, I introduced everyone to Gordon and explained the overall plan for the duration of our stay in St Mary's. It was nearly nine o'clock. Jack would, I said, tell them in more detail about what was planned for the next couple of hours. There would then be a late snack of hot chocolate and cake at about eleven o'clock. After that, everyone could decide whether to sleep or stay awake – as long as those who opted to stay awake did it quietly.

I then took the opportunity to remind everyone that the *real* purpose of the night's watch was to raise funds for the church repairs. Sponsorship monies could only be claimed, I added, if the watch was conducted in a proper and respectful way.

It may have been unnecessary for me to sound quite

so school-masterly, but I wanted to leave nothing to chance. I felt I had to make it clear that we were not all here 'just for a laugh'. Jack reinforced the point about general conduct, quietness, and the like, before outlining a plan of activities designed to keep everyone occupied for the remainder of the evening.

From then on things proceeded smoothly enough. Every now and again Edwin – sometimes accompanied by Adam – would slip away to inspect the space behind a pillar or investigate an area of shadow at the back of the church. But, on the whole, the scouts stayed together and did everything that was asked of them.

As midnight approached, Jack and Don gathered their things together, and I let them out of the side door just as the church clock began to chime twelve.

The door banged shut behind them in unison with the last stroke of the clock. As the sound echoed around the columns of the church, Edwin was once more to the fore.

'Midnight!' he said deeply and in a way that was full of meaning.

'Haven't you stayed up to midnight before?' said Gemma provocatively.

'Course I have,' said Edwin, clearly hurt by the insinuation.

'I think it's got darker,' said Adam.

'I don't think so,' I said calmly, wanting to dispel any superstitious thoughts.

'Course it's darker,' said Edwin in that strident way that only he could manage. 'It's midnight, isn't it? *Everyone* knows that it gets darker at midnight.'

He looked to Adam for support, but Adam was now staring at the floor and trying to distance himself from a point of view that he was unsure about.

'It's not *always* darker at midnight,' said a clear, deep voice. It was not Adam but Gordon.

He had remained largely apart from the scouts' conversation during the evening. Whilst Jack and Don had been organizing badge work and other activities, Gordon had spent much of the time quizzing me about my involvement with the church. How it had started. Why I had felt the need to become 'involved' in the first place. How that involvement had developed into what I described as a 'calling'. Why I had wanted to do the training. What being a 'non-stipendiary priest' or 'minister in secular employment' actually meant.

In response to Gordon's questioning, I had spoken as freely and fully as I could whilst, at the same time, trying to take an interest in what the scouts were doing.

During our conversation Gordon told me very little about himself. In fact, he had said very little at all, except to ask me a whole host of questions. I was therefore surprised when he suddenly spoke up to counter Edwin's misapprehension.

'It's not always darker at midnight,' he said. 'In fact, I've been to a place where you can see the sun at midnight.'

I could tell from Adam's immediately upturned face that he wanted to say something like 'Come off it!', but was prevented by respect for the burly and largely unfamiliar figure of Gordon.

'Is this a *real* place, or is it a riddle?' said Gemma, who was similarly unsure about Gordon's tone of voice.

'Oh, it's a real place all right,' said Gordon. 'When I was in the navy I was on a ship that was sailing round the Antarctic. During the summer we were staying at a place quite near to the South Pole, and that's where we could see the midnight sun.'

'I don't understand,' said Adam.

'Well,' continued Gordon, 'it's all to do with being at the very top, or bottom, of the earth. Within the Arctic or Antarctic Circles. That's when, in summer, you can see the sun even at night. People who get used to being there don't even think about it when it happens. They just get on with whatever their clocks and watches tell them to do. But the sun is still there at midnight during those months.'

'Spooky,' said Gemma.

'Weird,' said Adam. 'Tell us some more.'

'There's not much more to tell about the midnight sun. It really is as simple as that,' said Gordon. 'But I learned a lot about stars as well. Of course, I learned all about how they appear from the Southern Hemisphere, as that was where we were. But then, when we travelled back home, I was interested enough to learn about looking at stars from up here.'

Gordon talked for several minutes about the stars, during which time everyone gathered around him to hear what he had to say. The scouts were clearly fascinated by his talk of heavenly bodies, and responded with spontaneous enthusiasm when he said, 'How about we go outside and have a look at some stars? When I arrived this evening, the sky appeared to be very clear. A perfect night for star-gazing.'

'Yeah,' said Adam. 'Let's get out of this place. I don't think we're going to see a ghost anyway.'

'I agree,' said Gemma. 'Ghost or no ghost, this place is beginning to give me the creeps.'

'Let's go!' shouted Edwin. 'I've got my torch and we can play Lighthouse around the gravestones.'

I wasn't altogether clear about the details of playing 'Lighthouse', but I assumed that it would involve

163

shining a torch around indiscriminately and probably a good deal of shouting.

'Now, can I have your attention, please?' I said resolutely, determined to establish some semblance of order. The general hubbub died down at last, and the scouts looked at me with faces that said 'OK, but get on with it. We're out of here!'

'Now,' I said slowly and quietly, intent on not being rushed. 'In case it has slipped your attention, I would like to point out the time. It is, in fact, just after midnight. Most of the people who live hereabouts will be asleep by now, or very nearly at least. If we *do* go outside, it must be on the understanding that you all stick close together and don't go wandering off. You'll have to be *very* quiet – and I don't want that torch being shone all over the place. OK? Edwin?'

'What!' said Edwin argumentatively. 'No Lighthouse?'

'No Lighthouse,' I said firmly.

I thought that my conditions may have turned the scouts against venturing outside. Gordon, however, gave my admonitions a more reasonable interpretation.

'Michael's right, you know. And anyway, we won't be able to see the stars properly if we're shining torches all over the place. What we need to do is creep out and take up our positions quietly as if we were on the trail of something very mysterious.'

I couldn't help smiling to myself. Gordon had certainly won them over, and I was intrigued by the way in which he seemed to have transferred their quest for a ghost into an appreciation of God's universe.

'OK, then,' I said, taking my cue from the various nods around me. 'Let's go. Put your coats on. It'll be cold out there. And remember – stay together.'

With that, I led the eight scouts over to the large door in the south wall of the church, while Gordon brought up the rear. For our own security, I had made sure that we were locked into the church building, and so I had to slip the bolts of the south door to enable us to leave.

Outside the air was blowing crisp and fresh. There was an orange glow from the street lamps that lit the road between the church and the flats of Gracewell Court. A car drove past, and I could see the lights of a night bus as it moved slowly up the hill. Otherwise there was no traffic.

'There's a bit too much light here,' said Gordon as he looked up and down the street. 'We'd be better off round the back.'

So saying, he led the way around the west end of the building to the far side of the church where there were no street lamps or other lights.

'This is much better,' he said, sitting down on a bench which was shrouded in the deepest shadow next to the wall of the church. He motioned to the scouts to gather round him and I crept closer to witness the cluster of faces that turned towards the sky.

The next twenty minutes or so were a real education for me. Gordon pointed out the various constellations, explaining their names, how far away they were, and describing how many stars there might be that we could *not* see.

Throughout his talk the scouts sat quietly, staring at the sky open-mouthed, except for when they were asking acute and penetrating questions.

'How do you know that a star has died if you can still see its light?' asked Edwin, after Gordon had talked about stars 'dying'.

Gordon answered this and several other questions before he finally stopped. I shifted my position against the cold wall of the church, but the scouts made no move to go. Despite the cold breeze which was whipping around the side of the building, they stayed where they were, well wrapped up in their layers of sweatshirts and coats.

'I can't believe how big it is,' said Adam.

'It?' I prompted.

'The world. I mean, the universe,' said Adam. 'It's massive.'

'And it makes you feel so small,' said Gemma in a hushed tone.

Edwin nudged Gordon in the ribs whilst still gazing abstractedly at the sky.

'Where's God then?' he said. 'Where is *he*?'

Gordon smiled back at the scout. 'I think that's Michael's department, not mine,' he said.

'Oh, I don't know,' I said quietly, before saying more loudly, 'He's everywhere, Edwin. Absolutely everywhere.'

'He's bigger than the church,' added Adam knowledgeably.

'He's certainly bigger than the church,' I echoed, looking up at the dark walls from which we had just escaped.

'Come on, you lot,' I said, after a long silence had descended on the group. 'Let's get back inside. This wind's getting fresher by the minute, and I don't want any of you catching cold.'

With only a slight murmur, the assembled company hauled themselves to their feet, and began to tramp their way back around the west end of the church towards the main door.

It was just as we reached the south side of the building again that Edwin called out, 'Look! Up there. Where the light is. Someone's waving.'

All eyes gazed once more towards the sky. I was about to reprimand Edwin for shouting, but suddenly realized what he was saying. He was talking about the flats.

I looked up and across at Gracewell Court where only two windows were lit up from inside. At one of those windows on the second floor, a thin figure appeared to be waving at us.

It was like some kind of ghostly presence. It stopped us all in our tracks and, for a second or two, no one said anything. When the silence was broken, things seemed to move very quickly.

'They're not waving,' said Adam.

'It's Izzy,' shrieked Gemma. 'It's Izzy. She's in trouble. Quickly. We've got to help her.'

In that instant I realized that she was right. I quickly turned to Gordon and asked him to take the other scouts back inside the church. I would take Adam, Edwin and Gemma to find out what was happening at Gracewell Court. *They* all knew Izzy – and she knew *them*, especially Gemma. If she *were* in trouble, I felt it might add to her fear if she found her flat invaded by unknown people.

As we rushed towards Gracewell Court, stopping only to check the road for traffic, I tried to communicate to the other three that we should attempt to be as quiet as possible. We did not want to alarm Izzy unnecessarily, nor did we want to cause a disturbance among her neighbours.

Whether any of my young colleagues heard what I said, I do not know. They were ahead of me all the way, and I have the feeling that most of my words were despatched to another place by the urgent wind that was rushing down the hill.

So it was that they clattered in through the front

door of the block of flats, and up the concrete steps. To the first floor. And then to the second floor. Saying not a word between them.

I tried to catch them, taking the steps two or three at a time. It was a display of odd athleticism spurred on by a sense of panic. Although I did not quite manage to catch up with them, I reached the second floor landing just as they stopped about twenty feet further on, outside Izzy's door.

'Under the plant pot,' I called. 'The key's under the plant pot.'

Gemma reached down and found the key hidden beneath the terracotta pot by the side of the coconut mat. There was a brief interlude as she and Adam struggled to turn the key in the lock. In those few seconds I reached the door, just in time to join them as they almost fell forward, tumbling headfirst into the overwhelmingly warm, still atmosphere of the flat.

Gemma was again the first to lead the way into the small sitting room, where Izzy had turned from the window, her face showing horror and relief at the same time.

'Can't breathe,' she gasped, as she tottered towards Edwin and me. We managed to catch her frail body awkwardly in our confusion of hands, and we manoeuvred her light weight as gently as we could on to the chintz sofa.

'Open the window,' Adam called to no one in particular, as I put my arms around Izzy's body. 'Get some air in here.'

Edwin sprang forward and wrestled with the window latch for, it seemed, an age. Then, at last, a draught of fresh, cold air burst into the room and curled itself around our backs and into our lungs. It caressed Izzy's cheeks with a cool hand, and danced through her light, wispy hair like tongues of flame.

After a few moments Izzy's breathing resumed something of a pattern and she managed a smile.

I suddenly realized that I had been holding *my* breath. As I started to breathe again I looked up from Izzy towards Edwin. Past his shoulder, out through the window and beyond the night shadows, I could see the spire of St Mary's glowing in the light of a million stars.

I looked back at Edwin, noticing for the first time how frightened he appeared, and how the tears were beginning to stand out on his cheeks. As Izzy's breathing became more regular, I felt her squeeze my arm weakly. I gazed around at the others, conscious that we should ring for an ambulance or doctor.

Adam was standing facing Edwin, but staring down at Izzy. Gemma was kneeling on the floor between me and Edwin and staring up past my face at someone or something that was behind me.

I struggled to turn but Izzy lay across my arms. Then I heard a voice that put me at my ease.

'Michael,' said Josie, Izzy's neighbour and a nurse at the local hospital. 'Do you want me to take over?'

She moved into my line of vision, before continuing, 'And what have you been up to, Izzy? Trying to do too much again, I'll warrant.'

'Not at this time of night,' said the croaky voice that came from the fragile body in my arms. 'Just another funny turn. It was too hot. I'll be all right in a minute.'

Josie came over to the sofa and, in a very businesslike way, relieved me of my charge, whilst keeping up a nonstop conversation with her elderly neighbour. She explained how she had come off duty at midnight, and had been lucky enough to get a night bus almost straightaway.

Within five minutes, Izzy was sitting, propped up

with several cushions, sipping a cup of tea that Gemma had made, whilst Adam, Edwin and I sat around looking helpless.

As Josie went back out to the kitchen to try to find some biscuits, Izzy said to the scouts, 'You can talk to me, you know. I'm all right now, thanks to you. You don't have to worry. I'm not going to die.'

Adam, Edwin and Gemma remained silent, smiled a bit, and looked at each other in an embarrassed way. Then Edwin, feeling that someone ought to say *something*, regardless of what it might be, suddenly blurted out, 'Do you know about the ghost?'

Izzy looked understandably puzzled. Josie came back into the room with a packet of digestives.

'Ghost?' asked Josie. 'What ghost is this?'

'The ghost of a man who was killed outside the church when a bomb fell on it in . . .' Edwin came to a halt.

'1940,' added Adam.

Izzy looked at all the faces around her, and then started to laugh. Well, it was more of a protracted rattle really.

'When did you hear *that* old story?' she said. 'I haven't heard anyone mention it for years.'

There was another brief silence. We all looked at each other, and then Gemma asked, 'You mean you've *heard* of the ghost at St Mary's?'

'Well, I've heard the *story*, if that's what you mean,' said Izzy. 'Not for many years now. But I know about it. It started soon after the war. But there was never anything in it.'

'I'm sorry?' I said, feeling confused. 'There wasn't anything in *what*?'

'In the ghost story, of course,' said Izzy. 'Well, there couldn't be, could there? Because I saw him.'

'You saw the ghost!' exclaimed Edwin.

Izzy laughed again, her whole body shaking with the effort.

'Not the ghost,' she cackled. 'I didn't see any ghost. I saw the man who was supposed to be dead! The tramp. He was supposed to have been killed by the bomb blast. But I saw him, just down the road from here, only three days after he was supposed to have died. And he was as alive as you or me.'

'You were living here in 1940. Of course,' I said, stating the obvious, but only realizing at that moment quite how much of the parish's history had been spanned by Izzy's life.

'Oh, yes,' she replied. 'I moved into Gracewell Court just before the war started. When Mr Chamberlain was prime minister. I must be the longest surviving resident without a shadow of a doubt!'

I looked at Adam, Edwin and Gemma. The three of them were open-mouthed, and I felt I could guess what was going on in their heads. The realization that Izzy was *so* old that she had been here even before the war. That she had *seen* the man who was sleeping rough near the church. That she had actually seen him alive *after* he was supposed to be dead. That she had seen and done all that – and was still here!

In the end I couldn't help asking, 'Were you actually in Gracewell Court, Izzy, when the bomb fell?'

'I was here all right,' she laughed again. 'I was in bed. So was everyone. There was no warning. I think it was a stray plane on its way back from a raid on London, or so they said, getting rid of what bombs it had left. Of course, when I heard the bang, I got up and went to the window, much as I did tonight. The window hadn't shattered, as it was all done up with sticky tape. I remember waving to the air-raid warden as he arrived with the firemen. I remember calling out to them to ask if they wanted a cup of tea.'

I felt we could have gone on all night with stories about Izzy's past. The children were clearly fascinated, but I could see that they were also very tired. And, by now, so was Izzy.

Josie and I exchanged knowing glances, and I rose to my feet to lead the scouts back to the church.

'Come on, you lot,' I said. 'Gordon and the others will be worried about us. We need to get back to the church. After all the excitement, I think perhaps we'll try to get some sleep – especially as we now know there are no ghosts about the place.'

Izzy made no objection to our departure, and looked as if she was ready to sleep. She shook hands with all three scouts and made them promise to come back to see her again. Needless to say, they all declared their intention of returning at the earliest possible date. There was clearly more they wanted to hear about the man who was not a ghost.

When we arrived back at St Mary's, Gordon was standing just inside the door with the other scouts huddled in a group behind him.

'I was going to give you another ten minutes and then come over to see what was happening,' he said, his eyes responding with relief to our happy faces.

I clapped him on the shoulder and said, 'Thanks. I could do with a coffee. Let's get that kettle plugged in, and I'll tell you all about it.'

As I started to move towards the small kitchen at the back of the church, I felt a tugging at my sleeve.

'Michael,' said Edwin softly, his eyelids drooping. 'Can I go to sleep now?'

'Of course you can,' I replied, putting my arm

around his shoulder, and shepherding him back to where the sleeping bags and blankets were piled. 'I think we've all done enough for one night. It's time to rest.'

* * *

Our rest in the church was fitful. I remember sleeping for only three or four hours before waking to the sound of the scouts shuffling about around me. It had certainly not been a comfortable night, but it *had* been a good one. Quite apart from the rescue of Izzy – for that was how the scouts were now describing the event – there had been the lessons learned from Gordon and the dispelling of the myth about the ghost.

On account of my nocturnal exploits, I was excused the eight o'clock Sunday morning Eucharist, although I was back on duty for the main service at nine-thirty.

By the time I arrived home again at the end of the morning, I was shattered by the various activities and spent most of the afternoon sleeping soundly on the sofa whilst Amy watched *Fantasia* on the television and Cheryl marked essays.

On Monday morning I was back at work. As I prepared to go into a meeting about the advertising for a detergent with a new stain-removing ingredient, my colleague, Janie, presented me with a note.

'A phone call,' she said. 'While you were on your other line.'

I looked at the piece of paper on which she had written the following message.

'Isobel Hutchings rang to say she now knew the meaning of All Saints' day. Could you please say a big thank you to the other three saints?'

'All Saints,' I said to myself, chuckling. 'Of course.'

'All Saints?' said Janie, looking at me quizzically.

'Oh, it's nothing,' I said, remembering where I was. 'Come on. Let's go and talk about stains.'

Holy Orders

THOM BRAUN

From the moment he is stopped for speeding on the way to his ordination, wearing a polka dot clerical shirt and driving an extravagantly large BMW, it is clear that Michael Dunn does not fit most people's idea of a clergyman.

In fact he has a dual existence as a non-stipendiary minister and as a director of a busy London advertising agency where, to his great surprise, his gifts of ministry are occasionally called upon.

But life in the fast lane is a doddle compared to working in the parish where a redoubtable array of characters is brimming with advice for the new, inexperienced curate. Feeling more like a lamb led to the slaughter than shepherd of the flock, Michael's first six months at St Mary's are . . . well, eventful to say the least.

Thank goodness for Cheryl and five-year-old Amy, ever ready to come to the rescue and to keep everyone's feet on the ground . . .

The Sacred Diary of Adrian Plass Christian Speaker Aged 45¾

ADRIAN PLASS

The Sacred Diarist is back!

Certainly a little older, perhaps just a tiny bit wiser, Adrian Plass was amazed when his account of 'serious spiritual experiences' in *The Sacred Diary of Adrian Plass Aged 37¾* became widely read and appreciated as a funny book! More books have followed and now he's in demand as a public speaker all over the place.

Many of the characters we met in the first *Sacred Diary* are with us again. Leonard Thynn, loony and lovable as ever, has a serious confession to make. The Flush-pools, Victoria and Stenneth, are away on missionary duty, but we get to read their postcard from Africa and we hear about the most embarrassing moment in Stenneth's life. Gerald, grown up now, of course, is working with his Dad for three months. Why? That's exactly what his Dad is wondering. The answer is interesting, to say the least.

Adrian's wife Anne, voluptuous Gloria Marsh, Edwin, the wise church elder, and Richard and Doreen Cook are all back again.

The Sacred Diary of Adrian Plass Christian Speaker Aged 45¾ – another fabulous opportunity to enjoy the unique, wonderful and funny world that is Adrian Plass.

You Say Tomato

The Transatlantic Correspondence of George and Brad

ADRIAN PLASS AND PAUL MCCUSKER

Have you ever looked at yourself and Christians around you and thought: 'What a strange group of people we are'? Have you ever wondered if other Christians – even Christians in another country – felt as you do? If so then this collection of letters may be a comfort to you.

George, an Englishman, and Brad, an American, attempt to unravel the mysteries and sort out the cultural differences of two countries divided by a common religion.

They discover that the boundaries of stars and stripes, fish and chips, color and colour prove superficial at best, but deep down there is a common love and faith at the very heart of who they are.

Churches and How To Survive Them

RICHARD HOLLOWAY AND BRICE AVERY

Most people have a problem with the Church. Come to think of it, most people have a problem with Christians ... Why is it, when the message of Christianity is about unconditional love and acceptance, so many purveyors of that message leave others feeling uncomfortable and out of place? And why are there so many different churches to start with?

Richard Holloway, a bishop from the catholic, liberal wing who says he was converted by beauty, and Brice Avery, a psychiatrist from the evangelical camp who was won over by simplicity, meet for a few rounds of friendly banter. They attempt to get to the bottom of such mysteries as churchy behaviour, excessive zeal, purgatory, the seven deadly sins, the need for there being 'something more to life', not to mention the wholly avoidable problem of finding yourself brain-dead in Paradise ...

'What a fascinating book! It's like eavesdropping on latter-day apostles. A book that is serious and funny at the same time, it makes compelling reading for people with any religious beliefs.' *Joanna Lumley*

The Duffer's Guide to the Early Church

The tutorial notes of Michael Alexander

JOSEPHINE LAFFIN

Church history will never be the same again! Find out what the early Christians were really like in the company of Michael, Kirsty, Maureen, Christobel, Ruth, Frank, Wade and Neville – a fictitious tutorial group whose attempts at studying history are frequently hampered by their own Christian understanding.

'The members of the tutorial group represent all of us in our various attitudes and biases . . . with humour that made me laugh out loud.'   *Adrian Plass*

'Humorous and entertaining, yet pungent and penetrating, this little book is guaranteed to stimulate all those who might have found history to be boring!' *Clive Calver*

'Sugar on the pill!'   *Dr Meic Pearse, London Bible College*

The Duffer's Guide to the Medieval Church

The tutorial notes of Michael Alexander

JOSEPHINE LAFFIN

Join Michael Alexander and his fellow tutorial group members in the hilarious sequel to the bestselling *Duffer's Guide to the Early Church*.

Medieval church history is the theme for the new term, and with subjects such as monasticism, the papacy, heresy, medieval women and St Francis of Assisi to cover, there's plenty for the whole group to argue about! Two new students have now joined in the fun – how will they fare amongst the regulars?

In her inimitable style, Josephine Laffin vividly brings to life our Christian heritage and gently exposes our own presuppositions and prejudices at the same time.

'. . . learned, funny, clever and sensitive. This is history with a human face . . . If you ever thought the Middle Ages dull, or wondered where to start to learn about them, look no further.' *Rev Graham Tomlin, Wycliffe Hall, Oxford*

'Highly recommended as an entertaining and informative account.' *Rudolph Heinze, Oak Hill College*

'No history, of course, is dull, but if we ever doubted it, these discussions . . . would illustrate how the subject prompts people to show their true selves. The secrets of the tutorial revealed!' *David Bebbington, Reader in History, University of Stirling.*